The

TWENTY
DAYS *of*
TURIN

The
TWENTY
DAYS *of*
TURIN

Giorgio De Maria

Translated by Ramon Glazov

LIVERIGHT PUBLISHING CORPORATION

A Division of W. W. Norton & Company

Independent Publishers Since 1923

New York / London

Originally published in Italian as *Le venti giornate di Torino*

Printed in the United States of America

First Edition

"Nuova ipotesi sul canto folkloristico nel quadro della musica popolare mondiale,"
Alan Lomax, Nuovi Argomenti, pp. 17–18, Rome, November 1955–February 1956.
Used by permission of Odyssey Productions, Inc. o/b/o The Estate of Alan Lomax,
www.culturalequity.org.

"Phenomenology of the Screamer," Giorgio De Maria, originally published as
"Fenomenologia dell'urlatore," *Il Caffè Letterario e Satirico*, a. XVIII, no. 3–4, 1971.
Used by permission of the Estate of Giorgio De Maria.

"The Death at Missolonghi," Giorgio De Maria, orginally published as
"La Morte a Missolungi," *Il Caffè Politico e Letterario*, a. XI n. 2, April 1963.
Used by permission of the Estate of Giorgio De Maria.

For information about permission to reproduce selections from this book,
write to Permissions, Liveright Publishing Corporation,
a division of W. W. Norton & Company, Inc.,
500 Fifth Avenue, New York, NY 10110

For information about special discounts for bulk purchases, please contact
W. W. Norton Special Sales at specialsales@wwnorton.com or 800-233-4830

Manufacturing by LSC Communications, Harrisonburg
Book design by Ellen Cipriano
Production manager: Lauren Abbate

Library of Congress Cataloging-in-Publication Data

Names: De Maria, Giorgio, author. | Glazov, Ramon.
Title: The twenty days of Turin / Giorgio De Maria ; translated by Ramon Glazov.
Other titles: Venti giornate di Torino. English
Description: New York, NY : Liveright Publishing Corporation, 2017. |
"Originally published in Italian as Le venti giornate di Torino" |
Includes bibliographical references.
Identifiers: LCCN 2016052521 | ISBN 9781631492297 (hardcover)
Classification: LCC PQ4864.E583 V413 2017 | DDC 853/.914--dc23 LC
record available at https://lccn.loc.gov/2016052521

Liveright Publishing Corporation
500 Fifth Avenue, New York, N.Y. 10110
www.wwnorton.com

W. W. Norton & Company Ltd.
15 Carlisle Street, London W1D 3BS

1 2 3 4 5 6 7 8 9 0

Contents

TRANSLATOR'S
INTRODUCTION

IN A FAR-FLUNG CORNER of northwestern Italy, girdled by industrial haze, flanked by a crescent of jagged Alps, stands Turin, grandiose necropolis of a town. Baroque palaces, shaded neoclassical arcades, interwar military monuments and diverse hordes of bronze statues recall a history as the first capital of modern Italy and, in a fuzzier, earlier time, royal capital of the Kingdom of Savoy. It's a museum city, famous for its eponymous Shroud, its Napoleonic trove of Egyptian tomb treasures, its streets where Nietzsche suffered his tragic mental collapse. At first glance, a quiet museum city—yet museums rarely come without an odor of death, or, in Turin's case, a whiff of Armageddon. Nicknamed the "City of Black Magic" by its tolerant Italian neighbors, Turin has a long reputation for everything disquieting and spooky. Dozens of bookshops can still be found near its center selling witchcraft manuals, Satanism how-tos, UFO monthlies and the supposed confessions of ex-Illuminati. Walking along the River Po, you'll see bridge after bridge daubed with bilingual End

Times graffiti. (LORD JESUS IS COMING VERY SOON TO SAVE US WITH OUR FAMILIES, one reads, beside IL S. GESU STA ARRIVANDO.) By dread coincidence, Turin has also lent its Italian name to the Torino Scale, used by astronomers to grade the chances that a near-Earth object might "threaten the future of civilization as we know it."

Giorgio De Maria's *The Twenty Days of Turin* is a sinister, imaginary chronicle of the author's home city as it suffers "a phenomenon of collective psychosis." Written during the late 1970s, when Italy was tormented almost daily by terror attacks and police-state crackdowns, it balances apocalyptic fantasy with biting cultural observation. And while (we can all hope) the paranormal wrath he describes is pure invention, De Maria did not have to hunt far for scenes of a terrorized society. Wordless fear, determined amnesia and an aggressive impulse to *look the other way* are the story's cornerstones, and at least as chilling as its bizarre violence.

On its release at the end of 1977, the novel found early praise in *L'Espresso* and *La Stampa*, the latter hailing it as "a book dipped in the stream of cruel and timely metaphors." But trying times lay ahead. In the 1980s, De Maria experienced a sudden, almost Gogolian, crisis of art and faith, leaving behind decades of combative anti-clericalism to become a fervently traditional Catholic. Devoting his pen to religious literature, he struggled with depression and would produce no further novels in his lifetime. Meanwhile, *The Twenty Days of Turin*, his fourth and final work, fell out of print when its small, artistically minded publisher—Edizioni il Formichiere, or Anteater Press—closed in 1983.

Faced with these hurdles, *The Twenty Days of Turin* had a

significant gambit against oblivion: it was a book that fueled nightmares, and its cult status has endured among a shaken but grateful Turinese readership. One of the novel's major champions is scholar and critic Pier Massimo Prosio, whose *Guida Letteraria di Torino* remains the classic overview of Turin's literary culture—a hyperproductive milieu that can boast Eco, Pavese, Arpino, Levi and Calvino among its famous names. In the third and current edition (2005) of his survey, Prosio judges *The Twenty Days of Turin* to be "one of the most forcible examples of this starchy, formal city's capacity for stories of mystery and terror." Following De Maria's death in April 2009, Prosio wrote in the journal *Studi Piemontesi*: "As a storyteller, De Maria belongs to a rather peculiar and exotic tradition of Italian fiction, a writing that lies at the juncture of real and surreal, the blending of reality and imagination in a not impossible conspiracy." That style, he added, found its "most favorable expression" in *The Twenty Days of Turin*, "a proper *ghost story*,* hallucinatory and distressing, in the vein of the great horror masters, especially Poe." Equally, *La Stampa*'s obituary of the "reclusive and atypical" De Maria singled the novel out, many decades after it appeared, for its "image of a gloomy, disquieting Turin, stalked by demonic and violent underground forces which anticipate the reality of terrorism."

My own introduction to the book came through the mountaineer and music journalist Luca Signorelli, who first read it shortly after its release. He was seventeen; his brother Andrea was

---

* English in the original text.

fifteen. Their chief pursuits at the time were truancy, hard drinking, playing Black Sabbath albums and devouring French science fiction comics. They knew only vaguely who De Maria was. What professional critics thought of his work, or anyone else's, didn't interest them. Had some well-meaning elder suggested to them that *The Twenty Days of Turin* was "literature"—or (a thing more insufferable to their teenage tastes) "magical realism"— they might never have opened it. But like all wickedly memorable novels, it had a cold-caller's talent for snaring readers early, before they understood the finer writerly merits of what was scaring them to death. "Back then it felt as if your own backyard was taking some kind of twisted center stage," says Luca. Most of the original De Maria fans I've chanced into, from cartoon animators in Turin to ski shop proprietors in Courmayeur, were no older than the Signorelli brothers when the book was printed. Andrea Signorelli himself is now the front man of thrash metal group Braindamage. As an extreme mark of devotion, he lives in an Art Nouveau house in the same exact location as the book's first terror victim. He'd dreamt of settling there, he admits, ever since he read *The Twenty Days.*

Forty years on, the novel's fantastic elements have only crept closer to daily existence. Perhaps De Maria's most farsighted invention is a Church-run charitable enterprise called the "Library," created in a door-to-door appeal by a mysterious group of smiling teens. It consists of a reading room where citizens can donate their private diaries or browse the written thoughts of others. The Library does not accept conventional printed books.

"There's too much artifice in literature," the youths claim, "even when it's said to be spontaneous." They demand only "true, authentic documents reflecting the real spirit of the people." The Library's supposed goal is to help shy individuals find friends with similar interests and connect in "dialogues across the ether" after paying a nominal fee to learn the diarist's identity. Read today, in a world driven by blogging and social media, much of this sounds too familiar: diary entries on public display, crowdsourced amateur content, a new space promising emancipation to users who previously thought they were alone, even the infectious optimism that start-up founders brandish while pitching their disruptions. Without ever mentioning computers, De Maria has predicted the Internet's evolution better than many cyberpunk novels from the eighties and nineties.

Tellingly enough, the Library's patrons turn out to be "people *with no desire at all* for 'regular human communication.'" The institution becomes a colossal storehouse of memoirs by perverts and maniacs, taboo fantasies and even whole diaries devoted to bullying ("pages and pages just to indicate, to a poor elderly woman, that her skin was the color of a lemon and her spine was warping"). This collection of personal horrors—which De Maria often juxtaposes with images of garbage dumps and overflowing sewage—swells to mountainous proportions: "It had the variety and at the same time the wretchedness of things that can't find harmony with Creation, but which still exist, and need someone to observe them, if only to recognize that it was another like himself who'd created them." Worse, rather than helping its users connect, the Library consumes their privacy in a "web of mutual espionage . . . malicious and futile." Paranoid that anyone around them, friend or foe, might have read their unguarded confessions, the diarists are drained by an unnatural insomnia that sleeping pills cannot cure. Every night, they shuffle across the streets of Turin in a fugue state, congregating in squares, unable to speak to or recognize their fellow sleepwalkers. As they are crudely slaughtered in each other's full view, the insomniacs remain too atomized to react to the violence or describe the predatory entities responsible. And though the Library's initial form, housed in one location, is destroyed, it later reappears in a distributed network that covertly spans the whole city, as ineradicable as the Internet in real life. What is posted, alas, can never be *un*posted.

Being prototypical Turinese, De Maria's characters live under a code of repressed *dignitas*, a shell of stiff-upper-lip politeness—evoked locally in the phrase *"la tradizione sabauda"*—which both buffers and imprisons them. Tact is everything in their shy, buttressed world, while mortification is a fate worse than death. This leaves them especially vulnerable to the Library when it emerges to feed on their loneliness, and spells their doom as long as a fear of embarrassment exists. Profiled alongside his novel by *La Stampa* in 1978, De Maria remarked on these anxieties: "I want to say that Turin is not a neutral city. Even if you don't outwardly know anyone and no one knows you, you always get the impression you're being watched."

ꙮ

The narrator of *The Twenty Days of Turin* is an unnamed salary-man who lives alone, playing classical recorder and researching the insomniac massacres that struck his city a decade earlier. His attempts are rebuffed by fellow citizens who refuse to speak about the events and find their mention impertinent: some are even members of a Millenarist sect that accepts the killings as God's will. Ironically, very much like the Library's patrons, the protagonist himself is a lonely misfit searching for other individuals who share his forbidden interests. Though he befriends two similarly inquisitive characters—the generous attorney Segre and the part-time occultist Giuffrida—his quest ends in personal disaster.

De Maria, who began writing macabre fiction during the 1950s, shared certain vital details with his doomed narrator. "Earlier, I'd wanted to be a musician," he told *La Stampa*'s interviewer. "I have a piano degree from the Conservatorio. It was reading Kafka, reading *The Trial*, that forever converted me to literature: an epiphany, pure and simple . . ."

From his house on Corso Galileo Ferraris, De Maria would host salons, reading new material to guests and showing off his skills as a concert pianist. A frequent face at these evenings was Emilio Jona, who became one of De Maria's closest friends. Jona was Jewish, a friend of Primo Levi and a confirmed leftist in his politics. In 1958, alongside De Maria and other musicians and writers, including Umberto Eco and Italo Calvino, he formed the Cantacronache, an influential avant-garde music group that sought to revamp and politicize the Italian folk song. "Giorgio's personality was sparkling, lively, completely anti-conformist," Jona recalls.

"He was witty and entertaining." Jona made a curious contrast to the other regular of De Maria's soirees: philosopher and belle-lettrist Elémire Zolla. Unlike his two companions, Zolla was both a Catholic and a far-right thinker in the anti-modern tradition of Julius Evola. A prolific author, he would later become known for printing original essays by Jorge Luis Borges, and for his divisive preface to *The Lord of the Rings*, which endorsed Tolkien through a lens of reactionary Italian esotericism. His friendship with Jona and De Maria was possible at a time when Turin's intellectual culture wasn't viciously divided over politics.

In 1958, De Maria debuted his writing in *Il Caffè*, one of post-war Italy's top literary magazines. The published piece was a long story describing the 1995 assassination of a fictional "Pope Benedict XVI." It proclaimed his enduring interest in unreliable narration, alternate timelines and topsy-turvy parallel universes. Despite the work's anti-clerical sentiments, Zolla contributed a short, humorous note of introduction to be run alongside it, sponsoring De Maria as a new author to watch. The note concluded:

This is one of his long stories, or better put, one of his accidentally recorded digressions. De Maria's too fond of explaining his philosophical system in Piedmontese dialect, which will be an obstacle to introducing him. And that's an *add-on* obstacle to his scorn for the written word. His biography? He plays the piano and perhaps one day he'll see the publication of a "History of Godawful Music" from castrati to present-day keyboard thumpers. He graduated with a thesis on the shadiest heretical sects of the Middle Ages. He's tried to adjust himself to employment within various nationwide firms without success, because to a certain point his bosses could no longer manage to support the presence of a man so utterly harmless and insensible to the beauty of *"human relations."**

Old-souled yet iconoclastic, De Maria was a paradoxical radical who epitomized Theodor Adorno's quip, "One must have tradition in oneself, to hate it properly." Mass culture, like organized religion, at once unnerved and fascinated him. Raising his children without a TV set, he seldom visited the cinema but listened keenly to secondhand descriptions of movies his acquaintances had seen. While writing songs for the Cantacronache in the early 1960s, he became interested in the new style of jukebox rock sung by Italy's *urlatori*, or "screamers." As innocuous as these *urlatori* seem today, De Maria heard a dark and painful undercurrent to their music. The resulting analysis (included in this volume as "Phenomenology of the Screamer") shows his gift for drawing fearful meaning from mundane sources. Its account of "inward petrification," neurotic voyeurism and futile outbursts of "primordial, barbaric desires" suggests an early origin for the horror themes that would find full expression in *The Twenty Days of Turin*.

Much as Zolla presents him, De Maria held a picaresque series of day jobs. After serving as a wool merchant, he was employed

* English in the original text.

by Fiat in the 1950s. "Because he was a nonconformist and a left-ist, he was transferred as punishment from Turin to Brescia—this despite his first wife being the daughter of a Fiat executive," Jona recalls. "Giorgio was very absentminded and sloppily dressed and he'd get his jacket smudged with grease in no time when he ate. He told me that when his dossier finally came to light, one thing they cited as evidence of contempt for the company was that he regularly came to the office with streaks of talcum powder on his suit." Following termination at Fiat, De Maria became a theater critic for the Communist newspaper *L'Unità*, and—notwithstanding his aversion to television—also worked at the network broadcaster RAI-TV. Under commission, he wrote a teleplay (*Prova d'appello*) portraying a lethal dystopian game show. RAI-TV canceled the program but was forced to pay De Maria by a 1975 court ruling.

Pondering his late friend, Jona mentions the strange, oracular quality that ran through his stories of that era: "He described the [worker and student revolt of] 1968 before it happened; he prophe-sized the suicide attempt of one professor who couldn't stand the fall of his academic empire; he dreamed up, long before the big strikes at Fiat, a sexually motivated factory uprising."

Jona, trained in law, happened to double as De Maria's family attorney. De Maria fictionalized him in *The Twenty Days of Turin* as the urbane legalist Andrea Segre—perhaps the story's most val-iant figure, who embodies the better values of old-school Turin. "I was among the first to read the typewritten manuscript and the verdict I gave was entirely positive," Jona writes. "I recall that a character, the attorney Segre, was to some extent a portrait of me, and this is why, according to Giorgio, in honor of our friendship, he wasn't killed off."

De Maria's retreat into religion startled his old comrade, though the two stayed on good terms. "I recall that he publicly read out a kind of hilarious little tale describing this transition, and it was massively amusing to listeners who were unaware that he was truthfully recounting his conversion . . . His writing definitely lost its sting and irony, becoming flatly Catholic, but to a point, in his personal relationships, he retained some of his old contrariness."

Echoing his personal struggles, De Maria's fiction is filled with incidents of mental breakdown and talent cut short. The narrator of *The Twenty Days of Turin* treats his recorder as a reflection of his psyche, and it comes as an ill sign when he finds his usual joy in playing Bach has suddenly evaporated: "I placed my hands on the instrument without any certainty and breathed out foolishly like someone puffing into a blowgun." Another piece in this volume, "The Death at Missolonghi," depicts a shadowy force that robs Lord Byron of his writing ability. Decades before "impostor syndrome" became a household phrase, De Maria wrote this bleak description of private creative death:

It happens at times that men can outlive themselves and persevere, like wraiths, by carrying out the actions they have always carried out; their souls are mute but not their voices, and their hands and feet do not stop moving. Seeing them in the street or riding in the saddles of their chargers, no one would think that their minds had lost their hum, that the blood in their veins was heatless and spent; nor do the women they still hold tight to their bosoms ever imagine such a tremendous absence . . . And in the city there's no lack of them . . . Often even, the more the vacuum inside them is pierced, the more grandiosely they act, giving shows of themselves, fashioning great spectacles of gaiety, dauntlessness and brio. There's never a Carnevale in Venice where their masks don't make an appearance. And if times and manners continue to slide as they do now, it shall not be long before these walking husks will form great crowds, whose presence no one will be able to evade.

The scenery of De Maria's stories matches his protagonists' depersonalization. Even when the setting seems recognizable, there is always some clue that we're in a treacherous mirror universe where the hand of Fate lurks to gaslight the unwary. "The Death at Missolonghi," presented as a rambling letter from a bishop to a cardinal, carries an obviously false date, "the December of 1879." This befits its unreliable narrative, which puts Byron at the mercy of an elderly Venetian shopkeeper he has cuckolded. We're none too sure when *The Twenty Days of Turin* occurs, though its subtitle ("A Report from the End of the Century") implies that it's nearing the turn of the millennium. Our earliest clue that something has been displaced comes in the first chapter, where statues of Napoleon and Vincenzo Vela are described fac-

ing opposite ways from their real position in 1970s Turin.* Only
the book's first terror victim, addled by insomnia, seems to recall
their correct setting: "I could swear the statues of Vincenzo Vela
and Napoleon Bonaparte had swapped places. It isn't Vela with
his back turned on us, is it?" It *should* be Vela, at least in *our* reality, but this eludes the narrator, who later notices that two other
statues have traded pedestals across town without explanation.
"I thought that if I were a sculptor I would have made some corrections to the monument," he says. "Yet I had to admit that I felt
a touch out of place myself, even if I didn't know enough to say
what my rightful condition could be."

ﻌﻌ

The entities behind the book's carnage deserve some space of
their own. Giorgio De Maria's son Domenico has confirmed in
conversation that his father, writing *The Twenty Days of Turin*,
hinted that the novel in progress would concern terrorism. At the
time, Italy was home to roughly a dozen militant political organi-

---

* Turin's Vincenzo Vela Monument, designed by Annibale Galateri in 1911, now
stands at the T-junction where Corso Castelfidardo cuts across the northern tip of
Corso Stati Uniti. A bronze statue shows the sculptor Vela inspecting his master-
piece, a stone image of the dying Napoleon in his chair. During the 1970s, Corso Castelfidardo, which had not yet been extended into its present T-junction, terminated
at the monument, forming a sharp corner with Corso Stati Uniti. The Vela statue,
then, would have faced away from any real house on Corso Castelfidardo. However,
the novel's plot implies the reasons for such a "mistake." Before 1941, the statues
of Vela and Napoleon stood outside the Gallery of Modern Art on Corso Galileo
Ferraris—directly opposite the fictional location of Segre's apartment. The house
where De Maria hosted his 1950s salons lies two blocks away on the same street.

zations, from Marxist "armed cells" to clandestine neofascist networks. At least four thousand cases of political violence—some higher estimates run to fourteen thousand—are thought to have occurred during the "Years of Lead," leaving hundreds dead and thousands wounded.

The era's insurgent groups were far from homogenous. Left-wing radicals such as the Red Brigades focused their violence on authority figures and avoided indiscriminate strikes on the public. Seeking popular legitimacy, they explained their reasons for each attack in lengthy communiqués. While their favorite assassination targets were police and judges, the Red Brigades gained lasting notoriety with the killing of former prime minister Aldo Moro. Their violent strategy ultimately backfired, losing the support of their blue-collar base. Neofascist groups, meanwhile, waged a far bloodier campaign. Bombing civilian crowds in squares and railway stations, they caused the highest death tolls of any attacks in Italy's history since the Second World War. With few exceptions, they did not claim responsibility for these acts and—thanks to a now-infamous relationship with law enforcement and government officials—they went largely unpunished until the 1980s. Even since then, prosecution attempts have often ended in limbo. In the case of the 1974 Piazza della Loggia bombing, which caused eight deaths and over a hundred injuries, Italian courts only managed to convict two surviving perpetrators in 2015.

These neofascist terror groups suggest the most obvious human model for the "foul, small-minded deities" that threaten

De Maria's Turin. In keeping with their real-world counterparts, the entities remain forever untouchable, hiding in plain sight while authorities round up desperate, ill-fitting scapegoats. The narrator himself, when challenged, cannot find the nerve to name them aloud. Nor shall you hear the surprise from me. I'll only say that the entities' physical form evokes a very understandable Italian fear of the 1970s: that the past wasn't as dead as it looked, not even in a quiet museum city. As Segre the attorney laments, "It's very hard to rebuild anything when you haven't yet severed the serpent's head."

If De Maria had limited himself to writing a flat political allegory, *The Twenty Days of Turin* mightn't have aged as well as it has. His entities, however, have an odd feature to their hostility that makes them uniquely discomforting today. Before the massacres, Giuffrida and Segre accidentally hear them conversing and making horrific howling noises with "the intonation of war cries." Importantly, the creatures are not speaking face-to-face, but over the airwaves. Each voice reports what it sees from a blinkered, solitary position in Turin, and jealously tries to outdo the reports of its rivals. Even before they develop the capacity for speech, the nascent beings are driven by attention-seeking and one-upmanship: "Every now and then, a single voice would stick out from the choir, a metallic-sounding voice that seemed to express a clear desire to push its way through, to overtake the others stuck in their common effort." Segre has the impression that the howls, coming from "disparate directions," were "relaying some kind of message," but also "rising up *against* each other."

This hardly matches the old-fashioned terror of radical vanguards and synchronized cells, of insurgencies that counted on thousands of followers as a social base. More than anything, it resembles today's "lone wolf" terrorism, where no-hopers are inspired to copy the massacres of other no-hopers in a rolling wave of despair. Replacing a chain of command, we have friendless deviants who prompt equally friendless imitators far away through a sort of perverse quantum entanglement; the atomized lead the atomized. Whether he worships Breivik or al-Baghdadi, the lone wolf terrorist is a figure in Plato's Cave, called to violence by the currently trending shadows of other lone wolves. And like the Library users they slaughter, De Maria's entities have a frustrated, pathetic quality that they cannot conceal in their bragging. Never having met in person, they scream threats at each other through the unearthly communication medium that binds them. Their terror attacks are less a coup d'état than a personal contest for status, a status they initially try to measure in virtual quarrels over which of them is more privileged. Their rage, in short, feels wholly contemporary.

Finally, readers of a metaphysical bent may wonder what the entities precisely are. Is Giuffrida right in his theory that their voices represent society's "unconscious mind venting itself"? Or could they—as the Millenarist characters believe—be twisted angels sent to punish mankind, seraphs who happen to speak Italian instead of Enochian?

On its original cover, *The Twenty Days of Turin* reproduces a nineteenth-century lithograph by Félicien Rops titled *Satan*

Sowing Tares. A towering figure creeps over a city, one hand out-stretched, scattering his naked underlings from open fingers onto the scene below. Rops based the print on a parable in the Gospel of Matthew. In the story, Satan is an enemy who sows a farmer's wheat field with tares—toxic weeds that look almost identical to the true crop. Asked by his servants how to combat the infesta-tion, the farmer replies, *"Let both grow together until the harvest: and in the time of harvest I will say to the reapers, Gather ye together first the tares, and bind them in bundles to burn them: but gather the wheat into my barn."* Jesus himself later reveals that the parable represents Judgment Day: *"The field is the world; the good seed are the children of the kingdom; but the tares are the children of the wicked one. The enemy that sowed them is the devil; the harvest is the end of the world; and the reapers are the angels."*

It's apocalyptically fitting, then, that De Maria's entities sched-ule their carnage for July, the traditional wheat-gathering month on European calendars since the Middle Ages.

The motif has a local precedent with which De Maria was likely familiar. In 1821, Joseph de Maistre, the foremost Catholic contrarian of Turinese history, argued that it was symmetry and proportionality, *not lack of cruelty*, that confirmed the hand of an intelligent Creator. "If the plague recurred each year during July," he wrote, "this pretty cycle would be just as regular as the return of harvest time."

Like Maistre before him, De Maria imagined a Divine Prov-idence that was ruthless, opaque and, viewed through limited human eyes, seemingly amoral. *The Twenty Days of Turin* offers none of the cozier fears expressed in the phrase "... or the terrorists win." Nobody wins in De Maria's nightmare, where the Cosmos itself has become terroristic. It's open to doubt if even the Cosmos can reach its goals. The only safe choice available is not to pry too deeply. To paraphrase the novel's most fearsome mortal character: *Why insist on searching where human reason could find only shadows?*

But then, *someone* has to ignore such warnings, or else ghost stories wouldn't be ghost stories.

The

TWENTY
DAYS *of*
TURIN

•◆•

**A Report from the End of
the Century**

I.

INSOMNIA

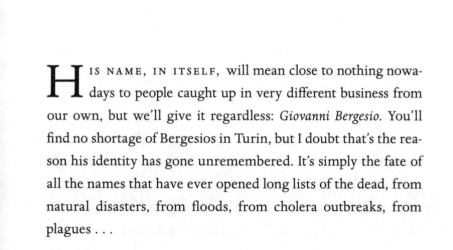

H IS NAME, IN ITSELF, will mean close to nothing nowa-
days to people caught up in very different business from
our own, but we'll give it regardless: *Giovanni Bergesio*. You'll
find no shortage of Bergesios in Turin, but I doubt that's the reason his identity has gone unremembered. It's simply the fate of
all the names that have ever opened long lists of the dead, from
natural disasters, from floods, from cholera outbreaks, from
plagues . . .

> Hence it was that this rumour died off again, and people
> began to forget it as a thing we were very little concerned in,
> and that we hoped was not true; till the latter end of Novem-
> ber or the beginning of December 1664 when two men, said
> to be Frenchmen, died of the plague in Long Acre, or rather
> at the upper end of Drury Lane.

So wrote Daniel Defoe in *A Journal of the Plague Year.* Who those two Frenchmen were who died in 1664, we don't know; it doesn't interest us to know and we won't quarrel with the English author for not being more specific. It's hard indeed to place epidemics by full right into the category of "historic events," as one does with wars. Whoever dies first in a war often enough has his name etched in history, and the same for anyone who has the rotten luck to die last, in the instant when hostility ceases. So what draws us to Bergesio, then, if the "Twenty Days of Turin" were neither a war nor a revolution, but, as it's claimed, "a phenomenon of collective psychosis"—with much of that definition implying an *epidemic?*

The newspapers had written about him on July the third, ten years ago, with much foresight, we needn't say, regarding the things that would follow. It was added that several members of his family were still alive and that it was possible to talk to at least one of them.

The dwelling where I now interviewed her was the same place where the victim had lived, and this aided our task of moving backward. The house can be found on Corso Castelfidardo, almost at the corner of Corso Vittorio, two places where the fury of those days was most unleashed. There to welcome me was Bergesio's sister, fiftyish and unmarried, with a ceremonious lilt to her voice. She'd scarcely heard the reason for my visit before dashing to fling open every room and every crevice of the house, all to make it understood: "The scene is exactly like the last time he saw it, before heading out that night!" Maybe our museums are as carefully tended as that apartment was. There was a smothering overload of objects, of knickknacks, nineteenth-century paintings, stuffed birds . . . A hothouse of relics that would soon be covered in dust and cobwebs if tireless hands didn't do their best to clean them nonstop. And Bergesio's sister was the only one in the house to generate that superhuman effort!

Just as she seemed ready to cast the most light on the past, with a flash in her eyes, she made me sit. I was struck by the fixity of her smile, the tautness of her neck ligaments, whenever she answered questions. She must have held beauty in her youth, a somewhat stiff beauty typical of certain English governesses, with a few features nonetheless that made her shape local beyond doubt. I surmised, after some broad questioning, that her life's philosophy led her to gaze with strong sympathy toward those esoteric groups who regard the "Twenty Days of Turin" as part of a providential design, a dire warning signal from on high addressed to humanity. She too, like the Millenarists, was a vegetarian. In the earliest days of her youth she'd already managed to pluck, from the living voice of the old Guru Krishnamurti, words she could no longer forget: "The truth can be understood only by an impartial mind, capable of detachment and serene judgment, pure . . ." And she continued to quote, for my benefit, selected phrases from the venerable sage. She seemed to prefer one word above all the others: *spirituality.* She uttered it often, and each time it came out of her mouth—naturally, to lament the shortcomings of modern man!—it resounded across the room like a faithful musket shot. Never did such a gentle mist of saliva cleanse my face as during those declarations of faith in the spirit! I tried to ask her if she'd happened to attend the "Library" a few times back in the day, but she blushed so much that I thought it was sensible to give that topic a miss.

Our spiritual, mature signorina seemed to strike up an elusive resistance when my questioning fell on her brother's last days. She preferred to skim over his adult life. In its place, she lingered on the happy times of his childhood, a childhood lived out with his family in a fervent communion of playtime. "When he died, Giovanni was thirty-five and not very satisfied with his line of work," she said suddenly in a hushed voice, tightening her lips and turning away her head. I had no time to get a foothold before she continued, forcefully, staring me in the eye, "Giovanni loved trees and flowers and nature! He had always loved them, since he was a boy!" It was like an injunction to believe whatever she was saying. I was starting to get used to the abrupt changes in her voice: sweet tones, almost velvety, when she drifted off into memories of the good old days, and an aggressive huskiness as she set out to impart me with several of her profoundest convictions. I still had a chance to get closer to the heart of the matter with a cautious encircling maneuver. I began to talk about myself, about my positively unexciting work. I told her I was working at a firm, that I loved playing the recorder and I'd written some books on municipal historiography. And then, little by little, I began to bring in the topic of insomnia.

"Did Giovanni suffer from insomnia at that time, too?" I asked her. She denied it. She denied it flat-out. Her brother never suffered from insomnia one bit! No, there was never a time when he failed to be well rested! She put too much emphasis on that story, and I gathered that she was lying. But I gathered too that she would rather die than admit to the contrary. Her declared love for nature, for flowers, her veneration of her brother's childhood; they all betrayed a stubborn desire to see "the beauty of things" at any cost.

And it wasn't hard for me to picture her manners a decade earlier, when the nightly city came alive with sleepwalking presences. I could imagine her "putting up a fight," the tendons of her neck pinched tight in agony, her spasms as she grappled in a deadlock with the impossibility of sleep. The categorical imperative of "spirituality" erected to prohibit herself from poking her nose out the door—to avert the shame of associating with other women who stooped to walking outside in their skimpy nightclothes. A victory was attained at the cost of a hermetic seal against the outside world; and the past, which was now fossilized, triumphed. Maybe she even resembled her brother somehow. I tried asking her, and she admitted it. Yes, she took after him in her love for the fine arts, especially painting. She went to get me some of his late tempera works out of a drawer: paperboard scenes of woods, of gardens, of farms, of a rustic landscape under a mild sky spotted with frayed cloudlets—nothing that would expose an outlook less than optimistic about the world. I learned that Bergesio had been employed at a bank.

"He didn't write much? Didn't leave a diary?" I asked. But the suspicion that my questions were edging once more toward the topic of the Library made her even more red-faced than before. I asked again if he'd said anything to her in the last days of his life—asked if they'd been on good terms. Now a tiny speck of truth came to the surface. Toward the end his behavior had become withdrawn, his sister confessed. It was all simple fatigue, of course, because he slept too little! No, one shouldn't confuse his sleeplessness with *that* insomnia—the one all the newspapers kept mentioning! Giovanni was different from other people. He lost sleep because he wanted to live in the country, to be a farmer, to paint . . .

"This was his real world here!" she exclaimed, flapping his tempera sketches.

"And that was why he couldn't sleep," she added to bolster the point. Her head gave a series of insistent nods almost as fast as a woodpecker. The mention of insomnia had left barely enough rapport between us to continue the conversation. On her cheeks I spotted the glimmer of two little teardrops: she sniffed her nose and quickly wiped them away. I had to be ready to jump on this moment of weakness.

"How he must have suffered, signorina, in those final days!" I urged, taking her hand. She turned away yet again, her head started to lurch back and forth and more tears sprang from her eyes.

"Giovanni hadn't slept for a week and he couldn't take any more. He had a weaker character than mine," she said, her tone of voice suddenly normal. "He said he felt very tired but could never quite fall asleep . . . He spoke of a very deep lake . . . Instead of stones at the bottom of this lake, there were bas-reliefs."

"Was the lake dried out?"

"Yes, it was a dry lake. That image was fixed in his mind: a lake with a very deep bottom. He said that even if the water came back, he wouldn't be able to fully immerse himself . . . There wasn't enough water . . . He felt that the bottom of his lake had suddenly been raised, as if someone, from below, had pushed it up . . . And that there was no real difference between the depth of the lake and anything else, not the city, not the asphalt, not this house . . ." Her accent turned dramatic mentioning the house. She wiped her eyes again and continued. "He couldn't fall asleep because he couldn't sink into the lake, and this even made him furious. He kicked the furniture! The chairs! And he used to be such a gentle person . . . Then eventually he calmed down, at least he seemed to calm down . . . "

I watched her spring up and pace across the room to and fro, clasping her hands in torment.

"But you still slept, signorina?" I insinuated.

"Yes, I slept, but I woke up often in the night and heard him in the next room fidgeting. His whole situation felt so . . . regrettable . . . Yes, it really did tear my heart! Sleeping pills couldn't help him; they couldn't lower the bottom of his lake. There was nothing that could lower it . . . I remember him talking about space, about room . . . He wanted room! He said that within him there was no room left, no more space to move, to turn around. He said something horrible as well: '*Even if I wanted to kill myself, I wouldn't find the space to die!*'"

"And then he went out that night."

"He left because he hoped that the streets, the squares, the avenues would restore something within him that had vanished . . . He thought that looking at the sky, the heavens . . .'"

She began to sob. I had to wait for her to calm down before asking about those bas-reliefs she had mentioned.

"The bas-reliefs? Oh, I can't remember well . . . He said that they were badly worn out . . . He seemed to recognize images of himself as a child and the faces of our mother and father . . . But then he wasn't quite sure: they were too weather-beaten, too eroded . . ." She gave a long pause, sighing. "I had no idea what would happen later outside, why I didn't try to hold him back when I saw him get dressed and make for the door. My place is here, in this house!" She said it proudly, with the tone of a vestal virgin.

"And what happened after that?"

"After? I don't know. I wasn't standing by the window to track him . . . He must have gone towards Corso Stati Uniti. I guess so, because they found him there the next day, next to a tree . . . I didn't have the courage to go and identify him. Our uncle went and recognized him from a medallion around his neck. I really can't understand what happened to him that night." She sat down, gawking at me with moist, curious eyes, as if awaiting a response.

"I think I might know," I ventured to say.

She tightened her corset, brought herself close enough for our knees to touch and seized me by the hand.

"If you know, why don't you tell me?" she said.

"I know he left around two in the morning, dressed to the nines, because his family upbringing would never have allowed him to head out in pajamas, as it occurs to numerous others . . . " She nodded eagerly. "And once he was outside, he came to Corso Castelfidardo, where he certainly found more people—other insomniacs like him. I don't believe that your brother tried speaking to anyone. He wouldn't have known what to say. No one spoke during that time."

"I know. He was a rather solitary person."

"He was obsessed by the dried-up lake, the bas-reliefs. He felt like he was being crushed by those images of stone and he was looking all around, searching for space. He was looking at houses, at treetops, at the stars . . ."

"Poor Giovanni!"

"Perhaps, watching the houses and the movement of the leaves, he tried to stir his imagination—who knows?—in an effort to loosen the grip of whatever was crushing him inside . . . That's when he reached the flower bed where he found the monument."

"The monument to Vincenzo Vela?"

"Indeed, yes. He must have stopped for a moment to look at it, unsure whether to proceed where the road curves or turn around into Corso Stati Uniti . . . His nose probably caught a strange vinegary smell, which at that time was fouling the air . . ."

"It's true, sometimes it came all the way here, even through the windows!"

"But it's likely he didn't notice: the vinegar smell had become an almost natural occurrence, especially for anyone living in the city center. Perhaps he took a walk around the monument. Has he ever talked about that monument? "

"No, but, well, yes! He mentioned it to me one day, half joking. It was to make me understand how his memory was starting to betray him because of insomnia. 'Alda,' he told me, 'do you want to know something funny? I could swear the statues of Vincenzo Vela and Napoleon Bonaparte had swapped places. It isn't Vela with his back turned on us, is it?' No, I answered him, I'm sure it's always been Napoleon's back, or rather, the back of his armchair. He shrugged his shoulders and gave a sad smile. 'Must be,' he said."

"In that case, it's likely that his torment was heightened looking at the monument. The gray figure of the sculptor and the white form of the dying Napoleon were very different from his bas-reliefs lying at the floor of a lake. They were sculpted in the round, and seemed almost alive by comparison. Prey to an inner anguish which had now reached its pinnacle, your brother made his way along Corso Stati Uniti. There must have been people on the street moving here and there, some crossing the road diagonally, others passing in straight lines. A few popped out from between parked cars, yawning and staggering: I can recall those nightly scenes well because I'd been there myself. There was something floating around, something ghostly. Your brother blended in with the rabble. Then, all of a sudden, I think he must have stopped."

"Next to the tree?"

"I couldn't say for sure, but certainly he stopped. His whole body must've stiffened. It might be that, hearing a noise behind him, the sound of footsteps, he still had the verve to turn around and see who was coming for him. But even if he saw, I don't think he was astonished. None of those people were startled by what was going on. It was a natural occurrence, like insomnia, like the vinegar smell. And then the horrible thing arrived which slaughtered him, as we both know: grabbing him by the backs of his heels and slamming him hard against the trunk of a conker tree. Whoever witnessed the murder made certain they didn't see anything. Was it fear? Indifference? And behind that silence, signorina, who's hiding the mystery of the 'Twenty Days'? It's for this that we find ourselves here, to discuss it, to try to understand—"

"Understand?" she shouted, shaking her head. "How could we—poor mortals—fathom the Lord's inscrutable designs! We have sinned too much in pride, sinned with our hearts, with our senses, forgetting that *spirituality* . . ."

She took away her hands and smiled at me softly. I sensed that she pitied me—pitied that I was still searching for truth with the limited means of the mind, when the way to reach it was so very different!

II.
THE NIGHT OF
MAY THE EIGHTH

T HE ATTORNEY ANDREA SEGRE, as we'll see, finds a place in our retrospective survey for reasons that are slightly complicated. His office and private residence are both located on Corso Galileo Ferraris, opposite the Gallery of Modern Art, on the second and third floors of an eigthteenth-century palace. It's a well-aired, leafy setting, which old folk remember with nostalgia for the days when they could tread across the avenues and not find parked motorcars getting in the way. Away from the boulevard, the property opens into a large residential area known locally as the "cottages," a jumble of structures with their private gardens spread out aristocratically between them. You almost don't notice the mixture of original styles and the by-products of the architectural imagination; at the discretion of their heights—two or three stories maximum—they very nearly blend into a single atmosphere of privilege. Cars are restricted here; only the "cottage" owners have the freedom to park.

When I entered the attorney's office, having made an appointment by phone, I was gripped with unease seeing the order that reigned in the room. A perfect arrangement of brown-spined books occupied three-quarters of the shelves in his library. In the remaining quarter there stood a *Treccani* encyclopedia, an entire set of *Ricciardi's Classics of Italian Literature*, some Bibles and books with Hebrew titles. High culture in full battle array!

I'd only just come from the Bergesio house, and the contrast was violent. Moreover, this wasn't a situation where you could have a regular chat with someone, sitting in two armchairs. Segre dealt with me from the other side of a desk; his sage, professional look demanded respect. If I had come to see him about a legal matter, everything would have been different. But how would I open a discussion whose starting point might've been a fleeting memory in the mind of my interlocutor? I covered myself by notifying him that my visit wasn't over any legal concerns, but I wanted it treated like a consultation—I had no plans to rob his precious time with chatter about a vague, dicey subject.

Immediately I sensed him cheering up by his wry smile, coupled with a keen, incisive look, as if he'd guessed the reason for my visit. Of course, it was impossible that he'd guessed. How could he imagine that his name had reached my ears through a complex game of hearsay, leaking out from friends of journalists who remembered seeing him enter the editor's office of a daily paper on the morning of May the ninth—rather shaken, it was said—to describe a strange nocturnal experience? He didn't think he was the only one who'd witnessed it, and wanted it reported in the news. The papers didn't run with it, but it was forever said that he'd insisted on carrying out a kind of private investigation in search of testimonies. Obtaining these, he'd return to the office—always in vain—after which he gave up and went back to his everyday life.

Segre offered me a cigarette and lit it for me gladly, then put a pipe between his own teeth, having fiddled at length with the bowl.

"Well, now?" he asked, looking down at me while his left hand stroked the hairs of a tousled, already graying beard. He had an aquiline nose, a slightly crooked one; it made him look like a hawk that had ruined its beak after nosediving badly into a mountain of rock.

"I'm writing a book about the so-called 'Twenty Days of Turin,'" I said, "and I'd like to speak to you to clarify a point."

He raised the pipe from his mouth and lowered his head, pressing chin to sternum. His lips drew back and his facial muscles tensed.

"Yes, by all means tell," he said in a strained voice.

"I would be interested to find out some more about an event of which you were—how to put it?—an *ear*-witness. I'm referring to the night of May the eighth ten years ago, if I'm not mistaken on the date."

He raised his head and looked at me again without smiling.

"And how would you know that I am—in your words—an

15

'*ear*-witness,' to something that would have happened so many years ago? Do allow me the question, out of simple curiosity."

I shrugged and arched my eyebrows, as if to let him know: *Giving an explanation that would satisfy you could be a bit of a challenge.*

My answer seemed to relax him. He returned the pipe to his mouth and relit it.

"I understand. In fact, I can't claim to have made any thorough breakthroughs, dealing with such a hazy, uncertain matter. I've groped around for something to make it less intangible, but, as you well know, all my efforts were futile. I honestly can't blame reporters for not giving weight to my words; even a serious and thorough attorney like me could be subject to short-term hallucinations—and I'm not ruling out that it was just a hallucination."

"An ear-hallucination," I added.

"Let's call it what we like. If you have any familiarity with English *ghost stories*,* you'll know that even 'ear-hallucinations' have a reputation around them: creaking chains, noblewomen moaning in castle towers. It's an old and venerable tradition."

"Yes, but in ghost stories, the hallucinations are finally revealed to be well founded: the ghosts are there for real."

"In castles! But which castles do we have around here? Castello del Valentino at the Polytechnic campus? Here we have the automotive industry, we have the ethos of central-city Turin, we have the commonsense citizen who represents perhaps the

---

* English in the original text.

solidest of our institutions . . . All of that would suffice to throw the most hardened army of specters into retreat!"

"We also had . . . the Library," I teased with a sneer.

"Even the Library can be included in the 'common sense' category . . . There, it's true, there have been some exaggerations, but—"

Rrrr-ibbit! Rrrr-ibbit! the office phone croaked. Without taking his eyes away from me, Segre chuckled and picked up the receiver.

I took a newspaper from his desk and began to read it: it's always awkward listening to the conversations of others, especially in the midst of client-attorney privilege.

Here, it felt Segre was trying on purpose to thwart me and slip out of our discussion. He spoke in a ringing voice, putting a special emphasis on legal terms like *statement of defense* and *letter rogatory* . . . Wallops of judicial realism, set to pulverize any speech I might have been assembling in my head. When he'd stopped talking to his client, he told me a vivid yarn in the spryest tone you could imagine. There was a poor husband who, coming home early, found his wife and his elderly father sauntering naked around the house—in front of his two-year-old daughter. Naturally, he demanded an explanation. So his wife sprang on him like a wildcat, shouting in his face: "What's this? You really had no clue that Roberta wasn't your daughter, and that your father wasn't her granddad like you thought? But where have you been *living* this whole time?" Now they were trying to shift custody of the child to the legal father, citing the mother's appalling behavior, and the case was in progress. Every day similar cases were happening, and it wasn't even among the most extraordinary.

"Small wonder too," he added. "In this city, demons lurk under the ashes."

"And so they did ten years ago, it seems to me . . ."

"Ten years ago, things looked different. It's better today. And yet, *the more things change . . .*"

"Would it surprise you, attorney," I asked, weighing my words well, "if you happen to hear again, on one of these nights, what you heard on the night of May the eighth, before all those other frightening events happened?"

He immediately noticed the little trap I had set him. Obviously he wasn't expecting it, though he was the one who laid the scene with his allusions to hidden demons. But it was too late to fix my mistake. So I found him in front of me as I'd first seen him on entering his study: hard and professional. I feared our conversation would be cut short, but it wasn't so.

"I'd like to make some things clear now," he said coldly. "The question you've posed to me is inappropriate. You're asking *me* for a wholesale explanation of those events, forgetting that *you*—and not *I*—are the one planning to write a book on the Twenty Days. Hence it will fall on you, and not on me, to find the connections between this or that particular happening. Let's suppose that, with effort, I managed to bring back an experience which appeared to me—I stress, *appeared* to me—as if it may have occurred in the past. Would you then consider me a helpful witness for your historical research? Fine, so long as you treat me purely as such. I don't plan to make conjectures about the future. So what do you specifically want to know?"

"A description of your experience," I said, guarding my tone.

"That's better. At least we understand each other. First, I might clarify that it wasn't the night of May the eighth but the early hours of the ninth. Indeed so! It was two o'clock in the morning when it happened, right as I was getting ready for bed after working late. I was tired but still clearheaded enough to distinguish sleep from wakefulness. I'm sure then that it wasn't a dream. As for those famous attacks of collective insomnia that struck the city that month, and were still in their early stages, I will say frankly that I've never suffered. Why? I don't know how to answer that. Maybe because I've always traveled a lot due to my work. My character was too elusive to be grabbed by that kind of epidemic, it being so very localized. But let's continue. I had just undressed, when suddenly . . ."

He paused, looking down at me.

"You know what usually happens in stories after the words, *when suddenly . . .* ?"

I nodded. His sardonic look returned.

"Something astonishing happens, without which the stories—"

"Wouldn't be stories," I said.

"Quite right, and there wouldn't be much worth telling, but instead I *will* narrate it. I said this ten years ago to journalists who glanced at each other, looking, we might say, a bit perplexed. I said the same thing a second time in the company of certain people able to confirm my version of events, and they proved to be even more condescending. Naturally, there wasn't a line in the papers about it, though I'm ready to bet that one of them must have *heard* what I, and others, heard that night . . .

"In short, I was down to my underthings, on the floor above us, where I keep my bachelor pad, when, suddenly indeed, I heard a scream. What's strange about hearing a scream coming from the street at two in the morning? A cry of terror might shake your every fiber and get you out on the balcony to see what's going on. The trumpeting of an elephant, blaring in the city, could perhaps have a stronger effect, but we're still in the province of acceptable things. This, however, was a very different affair. I had no words to describe the kind of scream I heard . . . Bestial? Inhuman? Yes, if anything, but that's still being rather nonspecific. I'd describe it like a terrible war cry, with something dismal and metallic at the heart of it . . . It's true. In fact, I didn't believe it was a person *or* an animal: it had an inorganic quality. I'm not sure if I can express the idea to you."

"And you didn't think that it could've been a loudspeaker?"

"That's a thing the journalists politely pointed out to me, but I didn't get that impression at all."

"And what did you do when you heard it?"

"Nothing right away. I stood there, thunderstruck . . . The glassware hadn't stopped quivering when a second scream, coming from a different direction but still close by, rattled me even further. It was the same type of sound: there was no comparing it with anything else, no label that suited it. Only it seemed to me that the second scream had a lower volume, like it came from a weaker throat—and yet it was extremely bold."

"Can you show me the direction?" I asked.

Segre got up, took me by the wrist and led me to the balcony. Evening was approaching; the motor traffic outside had gotten heavy. It was the side of itself the city displays in those hours: a flat, raucous daily grind.

"After the second scream," he said, "I finally decided to head out. The view from upstairs doesn't give much more than what you see here. There were some drifters roving about on the street, perhaps the first insomnia victims. I was struck by the fact that none of them seemed frightened. The only signs of unease came from the palazzo across the road, from *that* villa there, where a window was wide open: a fleeting apparition of a woman who glanced left and right, then quickly vanished, pulling back the shutters. There was an unusual smell in the air . . . "

"Of vinegar?"

"Yes, more or less . . . Anyway, I would say that the first scream came from over there, at the intersection."

"Near the monument to King Victor Emmanuel?"

"Roughly. The second scream came from the opposite side, from the area around the cottages . . . Of course, I couldn't pinpoint where exactly . . . Then a third scream, much farther away . . . farther away, and yet even more terrible. It seemed like they were relaying some kind of message. A few seconds went by, then other screams arose from the most disparate directions . . .

From this neighborhood, and then from lower down, lower down towards the city center, like echoes . . . And there was always something gray and metallic deep behind it . . . I repeat: they had the intonation of war cries, not only bold as I said, but virulent and hostile. Here, it seemed to me—though now we enter the field of subjective hunches—that the cries were rising up *against* each other . . . That they were not, in fact, directed at us, but towards the same entity that emitted them . . . That they were expressing a hatred alien to our feelings, but somehow, within the being of that hatred, we could recognize ourselves."

"Can you explain this contradiction any better?"

"Have you ever seen two animals fighting? Well, they do it for their own reasons, which don't concern us. Yet, witnessing their struggle, we can't help but feel implicated—by all the moments when we too, often as not, fight each other like dogs in the street."

"You mean, they seemed like premonitions of a battle that wouldn't have men as its protagonists, but other things?"

Segre gave a vague gesture, to make me appreciate that the query went outside the limits on which we had agreed. With a tender smile he invited me back into his study.

"The phenomenon never repeated itself?" I asked as he was closing the window.

"Nothing regarding it that I noticed."

"How many people, other than yourself, were aware of the screaming?"

"I managed to collect roughly ten reliable observers, all

people who lived in the historic center of the city. As far as I know, there haven't been any reports from the outer neighborhoods."

It didn't seem like our conversation would bring any further developments. I wanted to leave Segre my address but he turned it down. If, however, my investigation turned up any interesting results, he would be pleased to learn them. I was ready to say goodbye and thank him for his help when I saw him head toward his personal library and take out a slim little book. He handed it to me.

"This is Robert Musil's witty collection *Posthumous Papers of a Living Author*," said my host. "It's an old Einaudi edition from 1970, no longer in print . . . Keep it, and maybe you'll find something that will intrigue you."

It wasn't a book I knew. I assured him that I would read it with the utmost attention.

"Until we meet again, Attorney Segre," I said, shaking his hand.

"Godspeed!" he answered, meeting my grip robustly.

III.
THE LIBRARY

T HE REDNESS THAT LIT up Signorina Bergesio's face, at any of my hinting toward the Library, was a giveaway sign of a very common discomfort among people who live in the city whenever that special topic is broached. There's nobody anxious to remember the Library, except perhaps its creators—who nonetheless have managed to cover their tracks so carefully that interviewing them is close to impossible. But if you hope to paint an image of what Turin was like at the time of the Twenty Days, you cannot leave out the Library. How many regular clients did it see? Three hundred? Four hundred? Five hundred? Or even more than that? It's useless searching for the figures: all the statistical data concerning that establishment has been destroyed, along with most of the materials it held. How fast, almost explosive, its growth was! And they dismantled it just as quickly, at the order of the local authorities, ten years ago in September. No official reason was given. They proceeded to seize the Library's contents.

This material was eventually thrown into the incinerators, and, as far as I know, nothing survived except for a few notebooks in a house basement next to the Town Hall.

Still fortified by the encouragement Segre had given me, I decided to take the thrill of approaching some people old enough to have frequented the Library. I mixed in with a crowd at a market and, nearing the stall of a cheesemonger, I waited for the chance to strike up a conversation with someone. At random, I picked a woman who stood behind me with a huge shopping bag.

"Sorry, madam! Were you in line before me?" I asked her.

"Perhaps? I don't know. I wasn't watching," she replied, visibly moved by my courtesy.

"I think you were," I added. "But that's no worry. You can go ahead." She let out a sigh of thanks, and in all the time it took to place her order she never stopped making crafty glances in my direction, full of gratitude.

"Haven't we met somewhere before?" I said suddenly with a roguish drawl, while the merchant was weighing a piece of Fontina for her.

"We have?" she replied, startled.

"Yes, don't you remember? Quite a while ago!"

She tweaked her chin with two fingers and frowned.

"Well . . . maybe," she said. "I've always lived around here."

"No, no, not around here. We've met somewhere else. I remember you very well, madam . . . I'd see you almost all the time, on Sunday mornings . . ."

Her expression began to darken.

"You mean, of course . . . at Sunday Mass?" she stammered.

"At Mass, but not just there . . . You didn't by any chance visit the Library often?"

It was like I'd elbowed her in the gut. For a moment she looked at me, breathless, then promptly settled the bill and crammed the cheese in her bag, sidling away without even a *ciao*. Her reaction surprised me; it far outdid the blushing of Signorina Bergesio. Shooting in the dark, I must have hit one of her most nervous secrets. Other shoppers around us pretended they hadn't heard, though we'd spoken loudly enough. They gazed out at thin air, and I was certain that even if I wrangled with the cheesemonger for a quarter of an hour, none of them would ask me to speed things up. I saw some people creeping out of the queue. In a hurry, I bought two pieces of Paglierina. I wasn't going to increase the awkwardness.

This, and other, similar experiences, convinced me that upfront queries weren't the best way to approach my topic of interest. To make progress I needed a go-between, and so I was grateful when a friend spoke on my behalf to the current mayor. Thanks to his efforts, I had permission to go and rummage through the Library's remains. After that, I planned on questioning people who weren't as heavily involved with the institution, in order to expand my inquiry.

To reach the basement, with its stack of manuscripts that have survived incineration, one first has to clear the obstacle of two very suspicious watchmen who can hardly believe anyone would want to *study* such decrepit material. I don't know who put

them there or the reason why: whether their job is only to guard
the vestiges of the Library, or if they're charged with minding
other things as well. I do know that when I rang the buzzer on
the door, the figure who came to greet me seemed to rise from
an ocean of torpor. The other watchman was glued to his chair,
as if he and it were one substance. But as soon as they knew the
purpose of my visit, oh, my! It was like an electric current had
crossed them! Suddenly the unforeseen demand on their public
function ignited them with a bureaucratic frenzy rarely found in
those who fill such positions. They passed my permit around to
each other at least five times, examined it against the light, split
hairs over my documentation. (And *why* did I wish to go down to
the storeroom? And *what* was I hoping to find? But this was the
mayor's real signature? Did I know that I was the *first* to have made
this kind of request?)

"Well, go through! Go through!" they jabbered, after assign-
ing me a large rusty key that had been hanging on a nail. I took it,
a bit overwhelmed by their sudden change of attitude.

"Come along! What are you waiting for? It's the first door
downstairs . . ." With their thumbs they pointed to a spiral staircase not far from their desk. Then they fell back into their chairs
and didn't say another word.

I'd had the foresight to bring along two old gloves. I'd also
taken a pair of scissors and a flashlight, imagining plenty of strings
to cut and lots of darkness. I didn't encounter any darkness—the
cellar was lit by neon—but the rest outdid my worst expectations.
There was an unbearable stench of mildew and decay. The refer-

ence material was gathered in a single stack that occupied almost
the entire room: it made me shudder to think this mass of wastepaper made up only the slightest portion of what the Library had
once been. I recalled the library of Alexandria, whose conflagra-
tion had spared absolutely nothing. Here, fate had proven to be
milder: But in the name of what? It was hard to tell where to start
searching. There was also the danger that the whole lot would
fall on me like an avalanche. I plunged a hand randomly into the
mound and, trusting my left forearm to secure the treacherous,
shaky side of that structure, pulled hard enough to dislodge a few
odds and ends. It was a manuscript held together with string, plus
a couple of notebooks. I beat them against my knees, drawing
out a dust cloud that left me sneezing. I'd taken some occasions
to visit the Library and nose around the year it had appeared, so
I knew the spirit of these documents, but it pleased me just as
well to refresh my memory. The manuscript was made up of hundreds of rolled foolscap sheets that I immediately unfastened with
my scissors. The two notebooks were bound, one in green and
one in black. Each still had the reference number attached, but
the names and surnames of the authors were missing. Those were
the rules of the game back then. Readers who wanted to know a
diarist's identity could request it after making a payment to the
Library staff. Everyone's name and address was carefully cata-
logued. The writer of the foolscap sheets asked to be called "Evelina" and insisted that she was still an attractive woman, even in
her forties. Menopause had struck her too soon, she lamented. It
had wreaked havoc on certain "bodily drives." She was seeking an

understanding individual who could assist her, since her husband didn't want *any* part in satisfying her "new demands." He'd fallen to chasing younger girls. Now what Evelina yearned for was a young man who could spare his hands to help her defecate . . .

"I've become very constipated," she wrote. "There are days when my belly seems close to rupturing and I cry because I remember how I suffered during my pregnancy: I felt as heavy as a cannonball! Then one day a man in white appeared with rubber gloves and helped me unburden myself and I was so thankful, even if the kid was stillborn. Well, if someone came to my rescue now there are lots of ways I could show my gratitude. I'd pay them in kisses and hard cash. I won big at the football pools a few months ago and there's plenty of cheddar in the bank just springing to be taken out. I'm ready to give and give and give . . ." Page after page told of her torments and her need for liberation. One whole chapter was devoted to her bathroom reading: a hefty list of novels, newspapers and glossy magazines. Her appetites weren't choosy. Certain titles, though, were underlined in red. Next to a pulp romance by Liala, I found a treatise on semiotics. And another chapter followed, filled with descriptions of cutlery and silverware . . .

"If you really want to know," she wrote, addressing her imaginary reader, "I'm not the materialist you think I am. Deep inside me there's also a second desire, but it's so sublime I wouldn't be able to explain it unless we're speaking face to face. You would be proud of me if you knew it: it's the very purest of desires which shines like a soft light at the nethermost part of my being. Come and make it shine! You can do it!"

Toward the end of the manuscript, which I read skimming here and there, Evelina spoke about the feelings that came after the writing was over: the totality of the confessions she'd *poured out* of herself had given her a feeling of being drained, empty, voided, like there was nothing more to scrape from the bottom of her barrel—like *her riverbed had all dried out*. Now she was thirsty—and really wanted to get some sleep: "But thirsty for what? And what dreams could I nod off to?"

I remembered Bergesio's sister and what she told me about her brother's "dry lake," about those bas-reliefs. I wondered if this woman had ended up smashed to death along some city avenue. This was a purely academic question: "Evelina," for sure, was a nom de plume and the personal details in the Library's register no longer existed. It was fair to assume that, venturing from her house one night due to insomnia, perhaps half naked, she too heard footsteps behind her, and turned without wonder to see who was approaching her. Perhaps she gave a faintly curious, "Oh!"— one last automatic spark of vitality before even that ember was extinguished. Then two hands grabbed her by her lower limbs, swung her through the air and slammed her over the asphalt, or a tree trunk, or the body of a parked car. Whether or not she was among the first to die, used like a truncheon, against . . .

The revelations contained in the other two notebooks were more cautious. They spoke about satisfying some kind of poetic desire. This was a more elaborate language, trying dearly to package personal issues in metaphor. One work ended with a tirade against the despotism of the publishing industry; it seemed to have taken Vittorio Alfieri as its literary model. There were no references to parched lakes. Just a few allusions to the poverty of the human imagination and lack of initiative that was then plaguing the city. And on that point, the author wasn't wrong. I can remember quite well the "stifling atmosphere" that held sway over Turin at that time. The collapse of its industries. The exodus of immigrants back to their native provinces, which were at least safe from the severe drought that struck the entire Alpine arch. The overcrowded trains that left Porta Nuova station direct for Southern Italy, only to return half empty. New loads, new departures . . . The situation of finding ourselves thrust back almost at once to our indigenous wholesomeness—an event many "purebred Turinese" had even longed for with a sour regionalism—had ended up producing a general sense of loss. "Ah! Look who's returned! Now we're all in this together again, fingers crossed!" Among those who arrived to that fanfare, it would've been hard to find anyone ready to share in its joy. More often, they looked shrunken, secretive, ashamed. As it happens when you bump into a friend you haven't visited in decades, dressed by time in wrinkles and gray hair. Although the immigrants had left us holding on to their communal loose ends, so to speak, there weren't nearly enough battalions of pickpockets, pimps and hardened criminals to fill the vacancies that had formed.

The city authorities, at least some of them, had an accurate sense of what was coming. But how could the goodwill of a few handle a phenomenon which couldn't necessarily be fixed with superficial measures? It was vital (they said) to establish "community centers" at once! We had to stop new forms of "psychological alienation" from supplanting the old ones! The preventative action was extended to the whole district: *It was urgent! It was essential! It was a must-do!* How many papers were drafted, full of high-minded cultural intentions! How many mimeographed sheets were distributed among neighborhood committees! Yet the only "places of assembly" that were in any way functional were certain clubs mostly frequented by the elderly—ancient institutions like the Journalists' Circle, the Artists' Club, the Famiglia Torinese. Anyone who went inside, to view this anomaly in person, won't easily forget the haze of smoke through which you could hardly see the pool tables, the bridge players sitting like statues at their benches, the huge chandeliers of crystal that had turned opaque and—hanging over everything—that indescribable, unutterable, tomblike quiet! By chance, one bridge player broke hours of silence by accusing his partner of taking so long he was fossilizing.

"Fossilizing—me?" he answered.

"Yes, fossilizing! You, my dear boy, are a fossil!"

"So I'm a fossil now? Is that right?"

"Well, yes!" a third player butted in. "Everyone's always known the two of you were a couple of fossils!"

"You're gonna have it now—mark my word! Calling us fossils, indeed!"

And then there was silence again. Only the sounds of coughing and clearing of throats seemed to have the right to free expression.

Small wonder, then, that an institution like the Library found space to take root. It was presented as a good cause, created in the hope of encouraging people to be more open with one another. Its creators were little more than boys: perky, smiling youngsters, well groomed and well dressed, without a trace of facial hair. They looked designed to win people's trust. And who wouldn't trust a cheerful, articulate young man who came calling at your door, inviting you to chat with him about this and that, about the meaning of life, about all the hunger and suffering in the world? It's true; it was whispered that dark forces acted behind them, national and international groups hungry for vengeance after certain recent defeats. But who could believe such things in front of polite young lads who always looked you in the eye and shook your hand?

Their friendly chats ended with a humble invitation to collaborate in the establishment of a "library." It would be based in a hospital ward at the St. Cottolengo Little House of Divine Providence, a space large enough to hold shelves and a comfortable reading room.

"And what could *I* do to contribute to this?" their hosts would ask without hiding their astonishment at the proposal.

"Well, you, buddy"—the *you-buddys* flowed naturally from their mouths—"you could contribute by coming over to read, or bringing your own manuscripts, which will be archived and numbered and go towards forming the reading material. We're not interested in printed paper or books. There's too much artifice in literature, even when it's said to be spontaneous. We're looking for true, authentic documents reflecting the real spirit of the people, the kinds of things we could rightly call *popular subjects* . . . Is it possible that you've never written a diary, a memoir, a confession of some problem that really worries you?"

"Yes, now that I think about it, I *could* write something . . ."

"Very well, why don't you bring it along? There's definitely someone who'll read it and take an interest in your problems. We'll make sure to put them in touch with you and you'll become friends; you'll both feel liberated. It's an important thing we do, considering how hard it's gotten for people to *communicate* these days."

The monetary charges for "collaboration" weren't enough to deter eager patrons: three hundred lire for a chance to read, six hundred to know an author's name, three thousand for the acceptance of a manuscript. All proceeds went to the sole and exclusive benefit of patients at the Little House of Divine Providence. "As you see, this is also a work of charity. We need funds to improve care for patients, many of whom have . . . special needs beyond society's understanding . . . and rely on the hospital's free and confidential services. Divine Providence isn't an airy-fairy thing as we're commonly led to believe. Why, without practical assistance, who knows how many earthquake victims would still be living in tents . . . ?"

The optimism radiating from those youngsters, their whole-

some energy which ran against the historical mood, was the factor that went straight to people's hearts. "So when can things get
started?" people asked them. "For the time being, we're open only
on Sundays, but as soon as the initiative gets rolling, we hope to
stay open every day." It's easy to imagine what happened in those
households where the young men's proposal had been favorably
received: whole families (each member often oblivious to the
doings of the others) went rummaging in search of scrapbooks
that might've been forsaken in a soggy cellar. An old notepad full
of yellowed pages and frayed memories, suddenly rediscovered
and held up briefly to the light, regained a life that no one could
ever have questioned. It was read again frantically by those who
had written it. They'd notice the amount of things that had happened since the last entry—and hence the need to update it, to
buy fresh notebooks for adding new experiences. If the Library
needed "true documents," it hardly mattered much to dwell on
the structure. The pen could scribble freely whatever the spirit
dictated. And once it started, it was hard to stop! The prospect
of "being read" quivered in the distance like an enchanting
mirage—a mirage as real, nonetheless, as the "realities" that were
written down. *I will give myself to you, you will give yourself to me*:
on these very human foundations, the future exchange would
happen. Anyone hesitant to write could always save that privilege for later, after reading in the Library what their neighbors
had confided. If the weight of loneliness became unbearable, the
way out was well indicated: "Whose name matches reference

number [XY]?" The young man working tirelessly in the Library could reveal it, and the chance of establishing a correspondence was open at last.

I stayed up into the evening to trawl through those manuscripts. Upstairs, the watchmen were beginning to yawn and give signs of agitation. One came down to ask if I'd be at it much longer. In my hands, I had a dossier where a seventy-year-old, concluding a long diary, confided his desire to possess an eighteen-year-old virgin the same age as his granddaughter. I read through some ardent passages: "My dear, my delectable little girl, I'm still keen and equipped, don't you know? Every night at six, I go to Leopardi Park and sit myself on the bench that's near the myrtle hedges. I know that sooner or later you're going to read what I've written and accept my invitation. You'll know me by the book I'm reading: *The Heart of a Boy* by Edmondo de Amicis. My little heart is all for you! Come hither, little girl . . ." I heard the laughter of the watchman and threw the confession back into the pile.

The nature of the place where the Library was founded—a sanatorium rumored to harbor the pitiably deformed—had proven a lure to people with *no desire at all* for "regular human communication." I remember the case of a man who was normal in every respect, in words, in reasoning, in the practice of his profession, but strayed from this "normalcy" in only one way: his inexplicable need to fill thousands of sheets of foolscap paper with seemingly meaningless words, phonemes close to wailing sounds, cries of fury and pain in relentless successions, fragments of sentences and pleas addressed to God-knows-whom. All of this was so well organized in his memory that nobody he lived with could move one sheet from the piles that were growing day by day. The absence of a single page (felt immediately by his ultra-sensitive antennae) was enough to send him into a frenzy. The Library might've seemed like a refuge for a man like that . . . Everything could be deposited into the Library: works that were slender or unnaturally bulky, sometimes with a disarming naïveté in a world of slyness. Masterpieces could appear by accident, but they were about as easy to track down as a particle of gold in a heap of gravel. There were manuscripts whose first hundred pages didn't reveal any oddity, which then crumbled little by little into the depths of bottomless madness; or works that seemed normal at the beginning and end, but were pitted with fearful abysses further inward. Others, meanwhile, were conceived in a spirit of pure malice: pages and pages just to indicate, to a poor elderly woman without children or a husband, that her skin was the color of a lemon and her spine was warping—things she already knew well enough. The range was infinite: it had the variety and at the same time the wretchedness of things that can't find harmony with Creation, but which still exist, and need someone to observe them, if only to recognize that it was another like himself who'd created them.

When I came up from the storehouse I felt my stomach roiling. I returned the key to the watchmen and walked away with my head lowered, forgetting even to leave a tip. I slammed the door behind me. My research had barely begun and my ideas were still very muddled . . . Who knew if one day I could have returned to Segre the attorney and shown him those "interesting findings" that he would have been glad to hear about . . .

IV.

THE SECOND VICTIM

I N   A   T E N - Y E A R - O L D   E D I T I O N   (July 15) of the German
weekly *Der Spiegel*, there's a short article that's worth another
glance. It's an interview with a married couple from Stuttgart
who were passing through Turin in the early morning hours of
July the third. The tone of the piece is only half serious: the interviewer doesn't much seem to believe the couple's story. Rudholf
and Ruth Förster, for these were their names, had spent the afternoon of the previous day at the Galleria Sabauda and the Egyptian
Museum. After a light meal at a pizzeria they went to bed at the
Hotel Sitea at half-past nine. They'd counted on waking up very
early and setting off for Florence the next morning. They still
had images in their eyes of mummies and basalt statues from the
museum. Ruth had never seen such things before. She recalled
how she'd refused to have dinner at a rotisserie with her husband;
the sight of a grilled chicken put to mind the shriveled arms of an
Egyptian scribe preserved behind glass.

During the night, there were strange noises in the hotel that kept them awake: the sounds of doors opening and closing over and over again, the shuffling of steps down the hallway. Rudholf snuck a glance through the door and recognized a man walking in pajamas as the hotel doorman. His cheeks were hollow, his eyes surrounded by blue circles. He clutched his arms behind his back and strained, giving out cries, like bellows, which seemed to say: "Oh, God, just to sleep!" He wasn't the only one moving through the hall. There were four or five people, both men and women, all local people, perhaps hotel staff judging by appearances, stricken by the same madness. A woman in a very sheer blouse was making her way down the stairs.

Prompted by the interviewer to continue the story, Ruth said this: "So Rudholf and I went to the window to see what was going on outside, and even there we noticed strange movements, a bit like what you'd see in a hospital, or a prison yard during the recess hour, the same unhappy resignation. There were people wearing day clothes too, but they were so shabbily dressed that you couldn't distinguish them from the others. There was a uniformity that made your blood curdle . . . And to say how hot it was! Rudholf and I were drenched in sweat. The water was dribbling down from the tap. 'Rudholf, if I were you,' I told my husband, 'I would get out of here now.' He said, 'Me too, Ruth!' Having come to this, all that remained was to get dressed, pile everything into our bags and run like the devil to Piazza Carlo Felice where we'd parked the car."

"It was in Piazza Carlo Felice where you happened to see this . . . thing?"

"Piazza Carlo Felice," Rudholf interjected, "seemed to be the gathering spot for all those melancholy night-walkers. They'd form little clusters here and there but these soon fell apart as if their members had nothing to say to each other. Just as one cluster disbanded, another came together at a different part of the square, only to dissolve in turn. It was a kind of undulating motion; I don't know how else to put it . . . I had a vague feeling of danger. When we reached the car that was parked by the arcades at the opposite end of the square—a beautiful square, well lit, with trees packed with leaves and jets of water spurting from a fountain—we were still filled with horror at being forced to move through that crowd; they seemed high on Valium, or God knows what kind of downers. To follow the road signs we had to drive right around the square, a heavy task with all those vagrants getting in our way . . . We'd already done a half turn when, right there in front of us, we saw an odd character emerge from the arcades . . . Very far-fetched . . . Isn't that true, Ruth? He was gray-colored, stiff, with a severe expression, and there was something warlike about the way he moved. We hit the brakes to avoid hitting him and he went straight past us without bothering to look. We heard the sound of his heavy footsteps, like the clattering of a horse. These steps were vigorous and decisive; they made quite a difference to the shambling of the night-walkers who filled the square. We weren't just scared, but surprised; we couldn't believe how indifferent the vagrants were to his arrival . . . It seemed as if they were waiting for him, like they'd gathered there just to greet him. Ah, but that's not how the meeting went! There was no big celebration! Nobody seemed to pay attention to him, and yet, and yet . . ."

"And you, Frau Förster, what do you have to say?"

"Well . . . I must admit that I was beginning to get scared at this point. What scared me over everything else was the transformation this character was undergoing. Bit by bit, his movements seemed to get more agile. He snatched the air like he was catching flies . . . And he brought himself ever closer to those people, striding over benches, trampling flower beds . . . But rather than back away, they looked at him without batting an eyelash, like they'd all become rag dolls . . . Then suddenly one of them was grabbed . . ."

"And what happened then?"

"Ah! We didn't want to find out how that spectacle ended! I urged Rudholf to hit the accelerator, and, weaving through a daredevil obstacle course of vagrants, we got on the main road and swung straight for the hills. I didn't turn back to look. I'd seen enough thrills to promise myself that I'd never go back to Turin!"

So ended the interview. In the early hours of July the third, the very night *Herrn und Frau* Förster fled Turin, a thirty-seven-year-old woman, Rosaura Marchetti, was murdered in Piazza Carlo Felice in a way that closely resembled the killing of Bergesio. She too had her face smashed, two circular bruises around her ankles and deep bruises at the level of her midriff. With considerable force, two hands had grabbed her by the middle of her body and then—*hoopla!*—raised her high enough to take her by the ankles and spin her. The whirl ended with her ruthless obliteration against a solid mass. We should note that the "solid mass" into which Signora Marchetti was slammed was a monument this time, a memorial to children's author Edmondo de Amicis. Anyone who went to Piazza Carlo Felice on the morning of July the third to observe the "scene of the crime" will remember the mustachioed face of the Piedmontese writer, jutting from a slab of marble, still fouled with blood and gray matter, gory splatters from the victim reaching high enough to lick at bas-reliefs of children and the naked feet of the muse positioned on top of the monument. Signora Marchetti's death found possibly greater coverage in the daily papers than the demise of Bergesio. The parallels between the two crimes were immediately obvious: "A madman, a violent lunatic, prowls by night to assault our poor fellow citizens stricken by insomnia . . ." But who could that man be? From which madhouse had he broken out of? No sanatorium in Turin nor any other Italian city had any escaped inmates to report. Therefore, it could only be a case of insanity that had developed recently, and knowing this certainly didn't smooth the work of investigators. What a moving article appeared in *La Stampa* to express the horror and outrage triggered by the episode! The pitiless murderer had committed an unforgivable disgrace to childhood in choosing exactly that monument, that symbol of good nature, as an outlet for his fury! This was an individual *without heart*, whose case called for swift and vigorous action, followed by an exemplary punishment!

Unfortunately, certain obstacles that stood in justice's way proved thornier than expected. The autopsy attributed Signora Marchetti's death to the mashing of her brain, but there were unsettling questions about the dynamics of the murder, unique in the annals of criminology. Whose fingertips could have made the impressions found on the ankles and pelvis of the deceased? Who could have left such deep footprints in the flower beds of the park and the asphalt of the road? Human reason retreated in the face of such bewildering evidence!

There remained an inquiry into the victim's private life. Yet Signora Marchetti was a quiet homemaker, married, with two children (currently on exchange at a school in Switzerland). She didn't appear to have had any lovers. Her husband owned an industrial dairy and hardly needed the trifles he would've inherited as her next of kin. No private drama in the background, then. True, a man had suddenly come forward claiming to know everything about the murder victim, to have read her diary cover to cover, where terrifying confessions were written. "In my view, she completely deserved it!" he said at last. But when the commissioner asked him to be more specific, he could do nothing better than shrug his shoulders and mumble incoherently. Obviously, hot weather and insomnia were the real reasons for his meddling in the case; his pint-sized stature didn't remotely match the presumed murderer's profile.

They ran into a more serious obstacle when it came to examining the witnesses who had undoubtedly seen the victim's death. Anyone they found who was present in Piazza Carlo Felice at the time of the murder had no more to say than the people who were drifting along Corso Stati Uniti when Bergesio met his demise. Threats to arrest bystanders for withholding testimony came to no use. Whoever was there hadn't seen it, or if they had seen it, their visions of the carnage were too confusing. It was insomnia that had veiled the event; memories were clouded with fatigue and everything that had happened was permanently lost to absentmindedness. Until it came to questioning everyday citizens, legal threats, as always, remained a weapon in the arsenal of justice. But when the "upholders of law and order," the judges (and, it's said, even the president of the Court of Appeals), suddenly found themselves, not as *examiners*, but among the *witnesses*—and still couldn't provide the investigation with any valid leads—authorities became more willing to try the soft approach. They stooped to sweet-talk and flattery just to get a half-reliable answer they could work with. A reward of thirty million lire—with the guarantee of anonymity—was offered to anyone who finally came forward. It was no use. Only one clue was worth poring over: the places chosen by the murderer to carry out his feats. Corso Stati Uniti and Piazza Carlo Felice belonged to the "historic" zone of the city. As it later emerged much more clearly, those who committed murders in this way seemed to seek out distinctive areas deeply rooted in Turinese tradition. And it was just there, in those areas, where the greatest influx of restless citizens took place. What was the connection? Could all the facts investigators had gathered be helpful somehow?

V.
THE MILLENARISTS

IN MAYOR BONFANTE, I was drawn to a humaneness touched
by sorrow. The post he held, rather than filling him with self-
importance, appeared to make him droop: as if the heavy mass
of civic duties he'd taken on could flatten him at any moment.
How utterly different he was from Mayor Ambesi, who occupied
the same chair at the time of the Twenty Days! There, you saw
a brash, sanguine face, full of derring-do. Here, you had a pair of
sunken cheeks, olive-skinned but pallid, marking a constant inner
unrest. Bonfante spoke in a low, measured voice, like someone
who put lengthy and agonizing meditation ahead of each action.
His sharp ferrety face, when it wasn't crushed by a bitter wince,
seemed lit by a gentle, approachable smile.

"You'd like to hear something from me about the Library,
about its origins," he told me in his office at the Town Hall, where
I'd come, as always, thanks to my friend's negotiation. "Well, I was
a city councillor and I wasn't nailed then to the nonstop commit-

ments I have now. I had the spare time to follow the life of the city and see how it developed, and I certainly didn't neglect to delve into the byzantine workings of *that institution*—now thankfully dead and buried. I don't think the Library could've come to life if it hadn't found an accepting climate, a moral willingness to latch on to . . . We'll skip over the widespread tendency of many citizens to confide their worries in newspaper agony aunts and talk radio hosts . . . It's certain that from those media, things passed into a slimy subsoil, a drainage basin where anyone could tip anything they wanted, all the gunk they kept inside themselves. Have you ever seen something spawned from a garbage dump?"

"To be honest, no, I haven't," I replied. "But isn't it possible that the Library did reach one of its goals? To bring people closer together?"

"Oh, it reached goals! Quite a lot of goals!" he said with a dash of sarcasm. "But certainly not the goals you're talking about! Even those infamous contributions, those dialogues across the ether that were later purged by the Library, helped break that cycle of loneliness in which our citizens were confined. Or rather they helped to furnish the illusion of a relationship with the outside world: a dismal cop-out nourished and centralized by a scornful power bent only on keeping people in their state of continuous isolation. The inventors of the Library knew their trade well!"

A heavy silence fell between us. It seemed to me as if I could read into him and feel the gnawing anger that he dragged around behind him.

"So in that whole project you didn't see any twinkle of hope? Nothing that could have made you say: *It was a failure, generally speaking, but in one particular case at least . . . ?*"

"If you're suggesting a case where nonetheless somebody made a fruitful connection and got to form a friendship . . ." Bonfante leaned toward me, pressing the palms of his hands down on his desk. "Well, it could be that cases like that did arise. But what does it matter in light of everything else? The typical patron of the Library was a shy individual, ready to explore the limits of his own loneliness and to weigh others down with it. This only helped to seal him further in a vicious circle of fear and suspicion, which by long tradition have always hampered our citizens in broadening their horizons and communicating. Care for an example? Very well. Suppose that one Sunday morning a certain Mr. Rossi appears at the Little House of Divine Providence to peruse a manuscript. Having read it, he asks those charming boys who had the idea of founding the Library for the name and address of the author. They give it to him. And what does Mr. Rossi do now? He stands in the square near the house of the author—whom we'll call Mr. Bianchi—and waits, with the patience of a guard dog, for him to go outside. Mr. Bianchi steps out? Mr. Rossi follows him like a shadow: probably unaware that there's someone behind *him* doing the same thing, someone who's read *his* diary in the Library. And so, a web of mutual espionage came together piece by piece—malicious and futile. You couldn't leave the house anymore, take a tram, visit a public

51

place, without sensing the leer of somebody who wanted you to believe he'd soaked up all your deepest secrets. If I'd left any of *my* confessions in that place, I'd probably have lost sleep too . . ."

"So you think there's a relationship between the Library and the insomnia cases?"

"I never believed anyone who put the insomnia epidemic down to the heat, or the drought, or those toxic, vinegary fumes that were supposedly drifting through the air. If anything, *we* were the ones going rancid . . . But how?" Fervently, the mayor continued: "Do you think human beings are really like bottomless wells? That we can drain ourselves endlessly without sooner or later finding our souls depleted? In all likelihood, that's what people did believe, otherwise we would have stopped soon enough; but, unfortunately, we preferred to let the vampires drain everything, with the most extreme consequences. And so we saw!"

"Even the crimes back then, even the murders, according to you . . ."

"I can't give an opinion there . . . On that subject, we have to be very cautious. The one thing I can say is our city needs a total overhaul. It's a city which suffers from deep imbalances, with a giant, monolithic productive base but a spindly little head; huge lungs to breathe with, but a narrow windpipe which lets in very little air. Only now are we starting to break through a suffocating pall of abstractions, of hypochondria, which until now has formed the 'disconnect'—if you will—between the means and the ends of what we all hope urban life could be. It's an extremely difficult task. We have a century and a half of history behind us, from the

Albertine Statute onwards, conspiring to quash our initiatives. The dark forces that seek to hold us back are far from vanquished. All the same, we're beating them! We have optimism, willpower and no shortage of constructive vision on our side."

☯

Those last words from the mayor had cheered me up. I was in my car, driving slowly toward the house and taking in a beautiful spring evening freshened by an insistent sirocco breeze. The houses, the trees, even the people, had that clean, slightly immaterial tinge that the wind can lend even to the grayest industrial cities. I drove along Corso Regina Margherita and watched the unusually luminous cityscape that seemed to me like a general forecast of joy. People strode briskly on the sidewalks, though some stood around having avid conversations, gesticulating to one another. I heard laughter. Two kids got in my way on the frontage road, sneering at me. I responded by sticking out my tongue at them. One brat picked a pebble up from the strip and threw it at my windshield. I answered by sounding my horn in a marching rhythm. I asked myself what was motivating me to dig afresh into a past whose footprints, perhaps, truly were disappearing. Would I have been better off joining those forces fighting to give a new face to the city, instead of looking too far back? If I went back to Mayor Bonfante the next day and asked him to give me some task, however modest, that would somehow contribute to the rebirth of Turin, who knows how I might've been received . . . *You can start close to home,* he would've told me. *Attend your neighborhood committee, ask around, stay informed . . . I bet there's no shortage of work to be done!* Perhaps it would be best after all to continue plumbing the mysteries of the insomnia, the Library, those astounding crimes and that yowling Segre thought he'd heard.

I saw the Basilica of Our Lady Help of Christians looming to my left, its dome lit by the setting sun. It stood away from the main boulevard, in a sunken piazza at the end of a side street, appearing like a distant theater backdrop. I left the frontage road and turned toward it. This church had been one of the catalysts behind the Library's expansion. It was in its confessionals— dedicated to Saint Alphonsus, to Saint Philip, to the Great Mother of God—that invitations were whispered, for the faithful to join the crowd of manuscript-readers as "an act of devotion toward one's neighbors, a small sacrifice of oneself." I parked my car near the monument to Saint John Bosco and let myself into the basilica. The place was nearly empty: just a couple of old ladies kneeling before the main altar. In that silence that reeked of wax, where every little sound reverberated against the domed ceiling, my footsteps might've come from a lumbering colossus: they had a boom of discourtesy. Hands in my pockets, I gazed around as if I'd stumbled into a world completely alien to my usual routine. I was investigating mysteries, and yet the "mystery" that sustains a large part of our national life seemed to me, right then, unworthy of my recognition. I was annoyed simply by its clingy bombasticism. The two faithful old ladies worshipping on their knees were almost insubstantial compared to the statues of martyrs, the blue-and-white Madonnas, the gouged silver hearts, the wax saints in the side chapels, spread out on flower-covered bedding under sarcophaguses of glass. One of the saints, a nun, seemed alive. As I bravely approached her, I got the feeling that her eyes had rolled to meet me with a surly sideward glance.

I emerged from the church in no great rush, passing the door that led to the Chapel of the Relics, and climbed back into the car. Now I set out for the Little House of Divine Providence. Nothing was left there that spoke of the time when hundreds of people would queue at the entrance to carry out their pious duty as readers and contributors of written matter. Within the sanatorium's long, bare, prisonlike walls, life had gone back to normal as if nothing strange had ever happened. Moving shadows could be seen through the frosted windowpanes of a bridge that connected the Little House's two wings. The courtyard gates were already closed. A nun still lingered outside, her arms laden with bedsheets, the last duty she had to do before retiring for the night. I thought of an urban legend that swept through Turin when the victims were piling up at a frightening rate. It was said that the abnormal growth of the Library had forced the sisters to cut back on space for the inmates, to cram them all into fewer rooms, in monstrous amalgamations. In the deepest ward, which the eyes of strangers had never pierced, there lived a tribe of demented giants who were set free at nighttime. They carried out their carnage, then returned at daybreak, appeased . . .

My mind was flooded with turbid memories, so I decided to

cut the detour short and head back to my original route. Coming to the entrance of Via Cigna, at a roundabout where several streets link up, I chanced upon a crowd of people dressed in psychedelic patterns, including some conspicuous youths with long hair and shaggy beards—just like you'd see during the "protest era" thirty years ago. I was curious to know what they were doing. There was an atmosphere of piety; a girl squatted on the ground with a guitar in her lap and sang, backing up her vocals with scattered chords. The tune brought to mind some ancient litany. I parked my car at Corso Valdocco and walked down. Mixed in with the young people were adults who were dressed just as queerly. A woman draped in a turquoise sari waved at me and smiled. I responded to her greeting mechanically, and only when I looked at her better, after she'd already turned sideways, did I recognize her as Bergesio's sister. While a young man handed out pamphlets, the group of demonstrators made a half circle in front of a monument surrounded by an ornamental garden. They danced and tossed flowers at the lawn with nimble gestures. Pricking my ears to what the young woman was chanting so monotonously, I caught the following:

> *Here at Rondò Della Forca,*
> *Here, at the* "roundabout of the gibbet"
> *A kindly figure returns:*
> *The Patron Saint of the Hanged,*
> *To remind us that human justice*
> *Is ever in need of Christ's mercy.*

The meaning of this ritual wasn't very clear to me. An old man robed in sackcloth who had the air of a biblical patriarch raised his arms toward the monument as if imploring passersby to look at it. Now and again he lowered his head and joined his hands in a gesture of deep devotion. This was a monument showing the "Gallows-Priest," Saint Joseph Cafasso, giving comfort to a man sentenced to death—who, with his stunned expression and buckling knees, seemed anything but reassured.

The girl droned on, ". . . like a perfect scaffold between the domes of Our Lady of Consolation and Our Lady Help of Christians, shine the figures of Saint Cottolengo, Saint John Bosco and Saint Joseph Cafasso, who have rendered the name of Turin illustrious throughout the world."

I accepted a pamphlet and quit the gathering. This time I was determined to reach my house. The surprise interlude had left me unsettled. It didn't seem like the "Patron Saint of the Hanged"— as a *historical figure*—had really been at the center of all that gracious attention. It was the monument itself, rather, that seemed to attract them. Continuing to drive with one hand, I snuck a peek at the pamphlet. It carried the logo of the Millenarists and was full of urgings and rebukes, written in Italian, French and Spanish. Among the cardinal sins, after "sensuality" and "disbelief," it mentioned an "inattentiveness" toward "that which seems invisible around us, but is no less worthy of our concern."

"Take heed!" it said, among other things. "Unless you repent, unless you pay attention not only to yourself but also to *what you mightn't assume to be yourself*, the wrath of God, which can express itself *through all things*, shall newly smite you down! The 'Twenty Days of Turin' were the final warning of the LORD!'"

And in Spanish: "*¡Escápate por tu vida! ¡Huya de la ira que a de venir! ¡Ahora, o nunca! ¡Ahora, no más tarde!*" ("Run for your life! Flee the wrath that is to come! Now or never! Now, not later!")

I crumpled the pamphlet into a ball and flung it out the window.

Having just returned home, I got the sour feeling that I'd neglected some crucial task on my to-do list. But I couldn't remember what. I needed to eat dinner, smoke a few cigarettes, listen to Mozart's Flute Concerto No. 1 in G Major on my record player—in short, unwind—before a burst of memory gave me the sudden solution. I still hadn't read the book Segre the attorney had lent me! I searched in haste for my copy of Musil's *Posthumous Papers of a Living Author*, and at last I found it in the most unthinkable place: under the mattress of my bed! Why exactly had I stuck it there? Did objects have a mind of their own? With a sense of foreboding, I perused the titles in the Contents page: "The Flypaper," "The Monkey Island," "Fishermen of the Baltic," "Inflation" . . . And later, under the heading "Unpleasant Considerations," I found the subsections: "Black Magic," "Doors and Doorways," "Monuments" . . .

At that point, I stopped. The memory of what I'd seen on the way home compelled me to open the book at page seventy-five. And this is what the Viennese author wrote:

Of all the peculiarities that monuments can claim, one feature stands out for sheer irony: the strangest thing about
monuments is they're not at all noticeable! Nothing in
the world is more invisible. Even so, there's no doubt that
they're made to be seen, nay, to draw attention; but at the
same time they have something that makes them, so to
speak, waterproof. Your attention will run straight over
them like drops of water on oilskin clothing, never pausing
for an instant. You can walk along a certain street for months
and know every address, every window, every beat officer,
not escaping even the frequency of fallen pennies on the
sidewalk; but you'll inevitably be very surprised if, one fine
day, ogling a winsome female servant as she looks out from
the first floor, you find a memorial stone of considerable proportions, on which it's chiseled—in indelible letters—that
THIS HOUSE, FROM 1800 TO 1800-AND-A-BIT, was the home and
workplace of the unforgettable WHOEVER-HE-WAS . . .

Was this the passage that, according to Segre, was supposed
to fire up my curiosity? I read the rest of Musil's "posthumous
pages," but found nothing better to enlighten me. I imagined the
attorney's sarcastic gaze while I pondered what to ask him. Who
could guess how many things he knew but didn't want to tell me! I
had a wish to ring him up, but I was too tired, too muddleheaded,
to continue a conversation whose nature, by this hour, seemed
more burdensome to me than it was enticing. I went to sleep.

Late in the night, the telephone rang. I reeled to pick up the receiver—"Yes? Hello?"—but no one answered at the other end. Thieves, maybe. Thieves who hoped I wasn't home so they could come and rob me.

I ought to get the locks upgraded, I thought, going back to bed.

VI.
AN INTERLUDE

THE FOLLOWING MORNING, A Sunday, a friend I hadn't seen for ten years cropped up at my front door. I gave an "Oh!" of wonderment when I found him at the threshold, just as I'd remembered him: the same rosy complexion on his slightly childlike face, the same superfine blond hair, the same waggish blue eyes always seeking some occasion to sparkle with a well-timed joke. And this was an occasion indeed! He'd asked for it, coming to visit me like a meteorite, without a note of warning, which perfectly suited his harlequin ways. He was, after all, a Venetian who spent half his life thinking up funny stories just to tell other people and measuring how long it took for variations to reach his ears.

Eugenio Ballarin—so my friend was called—made his living as a flautist with the Teatro La Fenice symphony orchestra. Thanks to him, I'd learned the musical basics that allowed me to become an amateur recorder player—which, as yet, I remain.

Ballarin had already passed two days in Turin. But as for whoever phoned me the night before, he denied any involvement.
That would've taken all the fun out of his surprise visit: Didn't I
understand?

His singsong Venetian accent couldn't have come at a better
time. I loved listening to him describe how he'd spent his last
two days in the city: a jumble of details involving our own Teatro
Regio, where he was scheduled to perform solo next season,
along with some spicy comments about a songstress he'd become
acquainted with. "Why—oh, why—don't you ever come to Venice?" he asked me as we sat in my study. I told him that I fully
planned to make a visit once I'd resolved some minor business
here in Turin. My friend pulled faces. He didn't believe me: I'd
aired the idea of abandoning my city too many times already. If
I hadn't been successful ten years earlier, when I'd tried to high-
tail it out of fear, then there was no chance of managing now. I
was anchored here until my death! I think I turned pale when I
heard his merciless judgment. Perhaps Ballarin noticed, because
he broke away from that subject and suggested that we go out for
lunch to Maddalena Hill.

The hill—with its enormous statue of the winged Goddess
of Victory holding a beacon that pivots nightly in eternal memory
of our fallen soldiers—wasn't the best destination for someone,
like me, who dearly wanted a few hours to *forget* things. Below,
a vast and dreary urban area engulfed the flatland, and from
the clearing where my friend and I had climbed it looked like a
giant womb anxious to reabsorb me; it didn't move, but you felt

its immobility was a ruse. I preferred to leave that devious pan-
orama and set off with Ballarin along the trails of the neighboring
Memorial Park.

As we strolled through the woodland, Ballarin kept on stopping to read the names of casualties from the Great War, engraved
on bronze plates and fastened to poles struck into the ground.
Whenever he came to a plaque that announced an untimely
death, he'd say *"Poareto!"*—"Poor chap!"—in Venetian, shake his
head and aim rich profanities at General Cadorna's memory. It
was hard to escape the parallels between this kind of involvement and the "attentiveness" preached by the Millenarists. I wondered how *they* would behave in a place like this: Bergesio's sister,
those long-haired youths, the hoary old patriarch who'd accompanied them. I kept those questions to myself, since the gap that
divided me from my friend had grown too wide for me to fill it
by recounting my latest experiences. I liked it better when he was
talking, telling me things that had happened in his native Venice.

He told me a story that had me laughing with relish. This was
going back a while, to 1947, during a contemporary music festival.
The big-name composers of that era were Petrassi, Dallapiccola,
Ghedini . . . It was after the end of a concert, when the audience
had left the auditorium and the musicians were all heading to the
nearest eating house to fill up. But Ghedini didn't want to rub
shoulders with Dallapiccola, since there was constant bad blood
between the two of them, so he went his own way. Some instru-
mentalists saw him wandering through the dark streets, with his
head shaven like someone in a Greek tragedy, and followed after

him. All of a sudden the quiet Venetian night was broken by a
lewd barracks song. Hearing the barbarous cacophony behind
him, Ghedini quickened his pace. A pair of those musicians,
disheveled for the occasion, ran faster until they'd overtaken him.
Then they began to sing at the top of their lungs! At this point,
Ghedini tried to slip away, but he didn't have time to vanish in
an alley before another sound appeared behind him. *TARATÌTTA-
TARA-TÀAAA-RÀ!* He nearly had a fit; it was the theme for his
Trio for Piano, Violin and Cello, which had been played at the festival the night before. Ghedini thought he was dreaming. In the
meantime, as the musicians behind him kept singing their bar-
racks song in increasingly drunken voices, the ones in front bel-
lowed: "Long live the generation of '29, the generation of iron!"
And just then it resurfaced: *TARATÌTTA-TARA-TÀAAA-RÀ!* Now
Ghedini was struck with vertigo. They had managed to slip in his
Piano Trio so well that it sounded like a refrain . . .

"So now you know there are phenomena which can spook
even a modernist composer! Make him lose his marbles! With
God as my witness, that's my true word as a Venetian!"

Over lunch, when we'd already gotten to the fruit course,
Ballarin told me another story, which didn't make me laugh quite
so much.

"Do you know the baritone, Gi-*aah*-ni M-*aahn*-deli?" he
asked me.

"You mean *Gianni Mandelli*?" I said, correcting his yawning
Venetian vowels. "Yes, he's quite a good singer."

"A good singer, yes, but . . ." My friend puffed up his cheeks and held out his arms to show the circumference of the baritone's chest. "A walking howitzer like him could never fill the part of Don Giovanni; he doesn't have the trim of a seducer. You can't take him seriously when he's singing, '*Là ci darem la mano*,' let alone the sight of him in a duel. Now picture him in front of the statue of the Commendatore under a beautiful full moon. Right then, the statue starts to talk—and his Don Giovanni, instead of shitting himself, invites it straight over for dinner. When you've got statues that can talk and move around, it's no laughing matter! You'd need a will of iron not to lose your marbles! But directors don't think about these things, so much so that they've signed on Mandelli at the Teatro La Fenice to sing in precisely that part."

"So it was a disaster?"

"No, not a disaster, because the public doesn't even notice the inconsistency, and more, he *is* a good singer. But I did have the satisfaction of creating a little experiment . . . Shall I tell you how it went?"

He made a long pause, taking his fork between two fingers like a conductor's baton and motioning with it. Under his breath, he hummed one of the most climactic passages from Mozart's opera.

"Now that we're in a musical mood," said Ballarin, "try to imagine Mandelli as Don Giovanni, returning at night to his servant Leporello, all alone, not long after his fabulous altercation with the Commendatore's statue, onstage, if you understand."

I closed my eyes. "I think I can imagine," I said.

"Splendid! Now Mandelli is right there where you cross the

piazzetta with the statue of Nicolò Tommaseo, the sculpture nick-named 'the Book-Shitter,' and nearby there's a circular pedestal and on that pedestal another statue of a man. There are so many of those statues in Venice that nobody notices them anymore!"

"But Mandelli would have noticed that, surely!" I interrupted, quickly becoming nervous.

"Ah, if only! He wasn't onstage! Mandelli only notices statues that are onstage, and since there was no script telling him to notice them . . ."

"So what happened?"

"What happened was the statue suddenly gave a sound—*prack!*—like a great big fart. And Mandelli sprang around, only to see the statue fixed in its usual place. But still it went *prack!* The sound came straight from its arse: two times, three times, four times . . . And, my word! He turned white as a sheet with dread! His knees were quivering like *he* was the cowardly servant Leporello! At the fifth *prack!* he made a break for it like he'd seen the devil . . . And I was there, laughing my arse off on the pedestal with a terrible urge to chase after him. The next evening, around the final scene, I noticed he was a bit less festive and he even fell out of tune a couple of times before the Commander took his hand to drag him to hell."

It was a shame Ballarin had to leave that day. His manner of speaking—slippery and full of understatement—was the perfect medicine for me. Being around him, I found myself strongly nostalgic for a certain "largesse of spirit" that perhaps only came to me with too much hesitation: I'm referring to music and my recorder hobby, neither of which managed to absorb me enough that I could use them as a haven, a happy place to flee to in times of need. And so I could never pull my mind away from the demons under the asphalt, from the thrill of a chancy investigation. Ballarin, on the other hand . . . when the situation got too knotty for him, he didn't wait a moment to pack his bags and put his instrument in its case. That's what I saw him do a decade earlier; something in the air gave him the chills, so he kissed Turin goodbye.

Around midafternoon, I saw him off at the train station. I burned the rest of my Sunday by going to the movies, then I had a quick meal at a buffet restaurant near the river and close to my house as well. At eight o'clock it was already dark; I walked beside the riverbank and gazed at the lights reflected across the water: they made me think of long, phosphorescent lizard tails dangling into an abyss.

Before heading back to my house in Corso Casale, I stopped in front of the Gran Madre di Dio Church. A half-serious impulse had stricken me to follow the reprimands of Millenarianism and look at the building more thoroughly. At the fore of the neoclassical church stood a monument to Victor Emmanuel I: "King of Sardinia—returned to his people—the XX of May MDCCCXIV . . ." Guarding the church, from either side of its grand flight of steps, were two symmetrical rows of statues in white stone: two veiled women dressed in peplums with open books resting in their laps, each raising a chalice in her right hand, and at their flanks, two angels giving gestures of command. Having entered the church, I learned from a signboard that it was a work of the architect Ferdinando Bonsignore and inaugurated in 1831 before the royal audience of King Charles Albert. Under the shell of its dome there were niches where other statues stood, equidistant from each other: Saint Maurice by Angelo Brunelli, the Blessed Amadeus of Savoy by Caniglia, the Blessed Margaret of Savoy by Maccia. Looking at the life-sized features of the Blessed Margaret, a chalk-white nun with her eyes turned to the heavens, I thought back to Ballarin's latest anecdote: Mandelli the baritone fleeing into the Venetian night, terrorized by an unbelievable noise. What would I do if the Blessed Margaret hit me with a prank like that? Judder with barely controlled laughter? I made the sign of the cross and walked away.

As I came close to my house, I got a dim feeling that I was being followed. Quick, delicate footsteps. I didn't look over my shoulder because I found it silly to entertain certain suggestions. Already, I'd taken the key from my pocket and I was prepared to stick it in the door. And then my premonition became sharper. The gentle tiptoeing had stopped too. There was no mistaking it: someone was behind me! I turned around and saw a white figure facing me. I flinched as I noticed her extraordinary resemblance to Margaret of Savoy. No room for doubt here, this was a nun! The pallor of her face, nonetheless, seemed just human enough to calm me down a bit. I saw that she was smiling at me tenderly . . .

"I'm Sister Clotilde," she said in a pleasant voice. "And you are Mr. [. . .]? Is that correct?"

I nodded my head.

"I've been searching for you all day and I'm sorry to keep you out here in the street, but I would really like to speak to you."

"Speak to me?" I replied, sounding rather abrupt.

"Yes, to *you*! I am a sister at the Little House of Divine Providence. My fellow sisters have been begging me with such enthusiasm to find you and make a humble request . . . I saw that you were in our church a short while ago, and I might venture to believe that faith resides in your heart."

I held my tongue for a moment, none too sure where this conversation was going.

"What you mean to say," I suggested, "is that I have to change my life somehow? That there are certain vices, certain immoderate behaviors, that I have to give up?"

"No, no!" she said, her tone growing warmer. "It isn't your private life that's any cause for alarm! You're a kind person, sir, a good person. We would only prefer it if you showed more discretion towards those who now rest in eternal sleep—if, out of respect for their memory, you withdrew from probing into whatever reasons certain poor souls have left this Vale of Tears. We feel your concern over the deceased may perhaps be a little more worldly than Christian . . . I think you understand what I'm trying to say."

Nestled behind the sweetness of her voice I seemed to detect a somber threat.

"So in that case, I should stop wondering and seeking . . ."

"Never! Seek away! Wonder to your heart's content! Who among us could call themselves a child of God if they didn't ask questions, if they didn't seek new insights? So long as those questions are turned towards our inner life, to the soul which He has lent us! But why should we worry about unfortunates who have passed on? What makes it *our* place to know which ailment or whose violent hand tore them away from us? If their eternal fate is truly important to us, the Holy Mother Church has supplied us with every tool we need to help them: the powers of intercession, offerings to their souls in Purgatory, prayers! Isn't all of this enough?"

"For pity's sake, Sister, I know that! My upbringing wasn't short on religion!"

"What, then? If you, sir, are a Christian, if the waters of baptism didn't rinse your forehead in vain, why do you insist on searching where human reason could never find anything but shadows? The mercy of God is great, and if there are certain mysteries we can't pierce in this life, His Light will still be there in the next world to illuminate everything . . . Are you really so impatient that you can't wait just a *short* while? Make a *tiny* renunciation?"

She angled her head. There was a fine-spun ruthlessness in her smile.

"If that's all you ask of me . . ." I said, spreading out my arms.

"Why, what else could we possibly ask? What right do *we* have to interfere in *your* existence? The human suffering we break our backs over, night and day, is so measureless, so indescribable . . . It certainly wouldn't be the fate of a sane, able-bodied gentleman like you that would urge our care! You seem pretty qualified already to look after yourself . . . Oh, but I have no words for how happy I feel now, being able to notify my sister-nuns that you've agreed to follow their small request!"

It didn't appear as if she had anything more to say. She gave a faint bow, bent her knees and crossed herself. I watched her slink away as lithely as she'd arrived.

That night I found it hard to sleep.

VII.

The Voices

For a week, I went back to practicing on the recorder in my free time from working at the company; I started off playing scales, getting the hang of trills again. I wanted to make my fingers flexible enough to handle not just Bach's sarabands— those, I could more or less perform now—but also his gavottes and jigs, which presented far more of a challenge. I found no satisfaction in my imperfect renditions. I had to steer my mind somewhere else, away from where it had been busy until now, but woe on me if I irritated it with wrong notes, cracked sounds or other signs of insecurity; without a second thought, I would have read them as symptoms of a fractured soul and judged myself harshly. Was I looking for a haven, an oasis? True enough, but that oasis had to be gentle and flattering. *Tertium non datur!* There was no Option Three!

Why couldn't Ballarin be here, giving me some pointers? Right now he was probably in his studio with a grand piano and tripod stands full of sheet music, playing his flute as freely as a nightingale, maybe with a beautiful girl accompanying him on the piano. He'd mentioned it to me, in fact, that he planned to strike up a duo with a young lady pianist from Verona. A harmony of music and passion! *My* last memory of female contact, on the other hand, was Sister Clotilde . . . How could she possibly know about me, about my research? I could still remember the sound of her footsteps! *Tip, tip, tip* . . . I even had dreams about them at night, except in my dream it was Margaret of Savoy. She was a nun too, right? Putting that aside: Why did the sisters of the Little House of Divine Providence have to worry about what I was doing? What gave them the right? My temper was running short. On the recorder, my hands kept repeating the same dull triplet, while my mind took the opportunity to wander off into its usual labyrinth of winding side streets. "Come on, brain, be good for once! Come back here! Don't make me put you on a leash! Show me how to play this passage in tempo, without false notes!" . . . *Keep at it*, said my brain, *and call for me when you succeed!*

I thought that if the Library was still around, this might be a fitting moment to write down a lengthy confession and deposit it. I was in the right mood to do certain things. And to think I'd set out with the intention to write a neutral and detached historical inquiry! But in one stroke, a metaphysical hand had grabbed me by the scruff of the neck, dragging me back to ten years ago: *You wanted to poke your nose into things that were off-limits? Well, this is what you get!* Yes, but I was in no mind to go back to sleep right now, even when everyone else was drifting off. *Then put some effort into your recorder practice, learn to play it well . . . Work at the office by day, make lovely sounds with your instrument in the evenings and watch that you don't lose sleep . . . Don't give the sanatorium nuns any reason to pay you a visit . . .*

PIRIPIPI! PIRIPIPI! The phone rang. This was the third time already since I'd gotten back from work, so far with nothing but silence at the other end. If these were thieves, they should've gathered that I was at home by now. At this point, I hurled myself at the phone, dead set on giving this unknown nuisance a piece of my mind . . .

"WHO IS IT NOW?" I roared.

"Hello? Am I speaking to Mr. [. . .]?"

"Indeed you are," I said, "and who might *you* be?"

"Good evening! Perhaps you might remember me . . . I'm Segre, the attorney."

"Dear me, Attorney Segre! How are things at your end? Excuse my tone when I answered just now . . . I thought that probably . . ."

"Did I interrupt something? If you have company—"

"No, not at all! It's just me! Go ahead! It's nice to hear from you again!" I didn't ask myself how Segre had managed to track me down, since he'd refused my home address and there were plenty of names like mine in the telephone directory.

"I suppose you're working hard as usual on your book about the Twenty Days?" Segre asked me.

"Well, yes . . . On and off . . . Every now and then I take notes."

"But you haven't abandoned the project completely?"

"No, but . . . Well, it's a difficult topic, rather thorny."

"What did you think of the book I gave you?"

"Superb," I said, "very interesting."

"Have you read the parts about flypaper, about Baltic laborers? He's a great writer, Musil, one of the last truly sublime minds Europe can boast of."

"Yes, his intellect was extraordinary."

"Of course, it's not just about those passages I mentioned. It's a work full of ideas and sharp observations."

"I found the section where he wrote about monuments particularly . . . interesting."

"The part about monuments . . . And then the prismatic telescope . . . And Oedipus under threat . . . And finally, it's magnificent: the stories that aren't stories . . . Too bad for him that Vienna didn't recognize his talent; he was practically forgotten when he died. People only rediscovered him in the fifties. At any rate, I don't think they've given him a monument. For him, that would have been the worst insult!"

"That much I understood from reading the book itself."

There was a long silence. I wasn't sure if I was supposed to tell Segre something, or if he was supposed to tell me something. I heard him clear his throat.

"Do you know Mr. Paolo Giuffrida?" he asked me suddenly.

"No? Who is he?"

"He lives up in the hills. If you're still planning to work on the book, it might be a good idea to get in touch with him. He's an art critic, though he spends his free time dabbling in parapsychology, in the occult. But you can rest easy; he hasn't lost the plot, not like some of the chaps you see . . . I mean that he's a *serious person*. He's got some tape recordings that are well worth giving a listen to. Would it interest you to meet him?"

"Well, yes, but how should I go about it?"

"I'll give you his number and ring him myself in a quarter of an hour. That way, your call won't be unexpected . . . Now I have to leave you because one of my clients is here."

"I don't know how to thank you, Attorney Segre. It's very kind of you to remember me."

"This isn't a question of kindness. I've always had a soft spot for historical events. I thought it was only fair to give you some information that might be of use."

"Thank you regardless!"

"Ah, well . . . Good evening."

"Good evening to you too!"

It's always a tense thing, the gratitude you feel for people who, even with the best intentions, leave you standing at a crossroads. To one side of me, I had the gentle lure of the recorder, promising a life of peace and contentment. To the other, I had the name and phone number of a stranger: a beacon pointing in the dark, to a possible landing site nesting all the threats of the unknown.

Naturally, when a quarter of an hour had passed, I rang Paolo Giuffrida. He knew enough about me already that he didn't ask any questions and suggested I meet him later that night. Very carefully, he explained everything I had to do to find his home in a maze of narrow streets and paths. The house was located in a secluded part of the Turin hills; unlike the other owners of villas and cottages, my host seemed to avoid every precautionary measure that had become de rigeur in that neighborhood. His only safeguard against outside threats was the presence of a dog, which appeared immediately, barking at the gate of his little garden.

Paolo Giuffrida was a bony, pint-sized man of uncertain age, with a long face and a powerful set of teeth that made me think of a horse's head transplanted onto the body of a jockey. He sounded a bit snobbish, rolling out his *r*'s. Softly, he held his hand out to me at the entrance of the house, all the while stroking the dog, whose deep growls made me a little nervous. It was a young wolf dog with a coat of blond fur and answered to the name Gauguin: a docile animal, by all appearances, who immediately began to rub his muzzle against my trousers and sniff at my shoes.

The house, garden and furnishings all seemed to provide the requisite living space where a man of Giuffrida's proportions could live at ease without wasting a move. This was the calculated habitat of a "person of taste," receptive to modernity but tempered by coquettish links to the past: beanbag seats in blazing colors, African masks, sculptures of what appeared to be snout-beetles, cutting-edge radio equipment and instrument panels, all flawlessly coexisting with Napoleonic furniture, a Cignaroli landscape, a statue of Diana the Huntress positioned in the garden, Pre-Raphaelite etchings . . .

Caught in the middle of that erudite collection of past and present, I could only greet my host with an absentminded, "Good evening," as I gawked helplessly at the scene around me. All of this must have seemed quite natural to Giuffrida. Before getting on to the crucial issues, he made a series of smiles at me and the dog in equal measure. He'd glance back at the garden swaddled in darkness, giving distracted gestures that might've delayed our entry into the house for God knows how long. It was Gauguin who thought to break the deadlock, rising up and leaning his front paws against me from behind. "Get away, Gauguin! Atta-boy!" his master ordered, and the dog obediently went and huddled in a corner. By Giuffrida's own design, the ground floor of the cottage consisted of a single room. Alongside the visual niceties, there were plenty of things to hear and smell: the aroma of Indian joss sticks, a thin-spread and barely audible harpsichord music in which I recognized the notes of Handel's "The Harmonious Blacksmith." If my host was—as Segre had claimed—someone who engaged himself in parapsychology and the occult, then he kept those interests very well disguised. Nothing in the immediate environment seemed to betray inclinations outside the mainstream culture. When at last I found myself submerged in a beanbag, with Giuffrida lying on the moquette in front of me, the sense of physical comfort that swept over me was so total that I wondered in earnest if I'd come to the wrong address. I'd always thought that stiff, angular chains and rooms bathed in twilight were essential ingredients in the beckoning of phantom presences and otherworldly voices.

But soon enough we arrived at our main topic. Giuffrida restated briefly what he knew about me and the book I planned

to write, and explained to me that his "extraprofessional interests" should not be confused with certain pseudosciences of an
esoteric nature—spirit-channeling, mesmerism, attempts at telepathic contact with aliens and so forth. All of those pursuits were
standard fare for the Archaeopteryx Club, that white collar coven
of man-Fridays, bored office rats and petty lawyers aching for
mystical nostalgia; a few hours of well-applied eroticism and their
itch would be scratched. Giuffrida, on the other hand—in the
spare time when the art galleries allowed him a few moments'
cease-fire—had the hobby of tape-recording "acoustic manifestations," sounds whose sources couldn't be identified. His activity
was entirely neutral and unbiased, and didn't require gifts beyond
the human norm. In short, and to avoid misunderstanding, he
was *not* the psychic heir to the fabulous Gustavo Rol!

"Perhaps your experiments have something in common
with those 'voices of the deceased' recordings from back in the
day—the ones by Jürgenson and Konstantin Raudive?" I asked,
fascinated.

"Yes . . . But with the difference that—in face of certain
phenomena—Jürgenson, Raudive and their whole school are
firmly perched on a spiritualist position, while I'm a bit more hesitant to drag the afterlife into all of this. If anything, I lean more
towards Hans Bender's hypothesis that what we call 'apparitions'
aren't ghosts but the unconscious mind venting itself . . . I imagine that the attorney Segre has spoken about some of my recordings that could address the topic you're dealing with."

"Yes, he mentioned that over the phone—in a rather fuzzy way."

"Fuzzy?" asked a surprised Giuffrida. "Well, then I'll have to clarify some matters before you listen to anything. The tape I've set aside for you contains sounds of an entirely different nature from what Raudive picked up. Let's be clear on this. It has *nothing* to do with any 'voices from the hereafter,' which anyone can tape at any time: even now, if you and I were to make the effort. The voices I've captured—which I've managed to keep well nigh unaltered by virtue of a tape preservation device patented by me—go back ten years ago; their like has never reappeared since then. It's a unique document. Indeed, I'd politely ask you to keep your mouth zipped about this, since I haven't ruled out that there are people who might come and seize it if they knew it existed."

I gave Giuffrida my most fervent assurance.

"Please, I was not joking! I'm asking you to keep this absolutely confidential!" I wasn't sure if there was real fear behind Giuffrida's entreaties, or if it was a histrionic stunt to give the recording a touch of mystery. I watched him get up and thrust his hand into a shelf to remove an egg-shaped object. Then I saw him glance around suspiciously, opening the door to take a look at the garden and closing it again with two turns of the key. When he returned to me, his face was agitated and constantly twitching. He inserted the object into an apparatus hidden behind a curtain, and before he hit "Play," he lingered on some technical explanations: the "voices" I was going to hear hadn't been captured by the tape recorder itself but by a two-way radio transceiver. He'd picked them up one night by accident, before they even revealed themselves as voices. At that point, they were simply noises—strange noises that immediately filled him with curiosity. This event dated back to April of ten years ago. He thought at first that it was a backyard hoax by some radio hams. But the persistence of the noises, night after night, and their gradual transformation into lucid words—albeit in an utterly bizarre timbre—before they finally swelled into "acoustic manifestations," which were astonishing to say the least, left him persuaded that the phenomenon was authentic.

Giuffrida decided not to say any more and to leave me to my own opinions. We could swap thoughts afterward. He pushed a button and explained, as the tape began running, that the egg-shaped cassette contained audio collected across an entire month. It would take us at least two days to listen to all of it, so, for my benefit, he would only select some essential parts.

After a long minute of scratchy silence, I became aware of a faint chiseling sound, a deep, rhythmic pitter-patter, close to the sound a workman might produce trying to engrave something onto a rock. It was joined by other chiseling noises, until everything formed a remote but hectic soundscape, like an underground mining operation, accompanied by wheezing and something that resembled a heart pulsating under a stethoscope. As the sound of magma slowly increased and thickened, Gauguin, who up to that moment had stayed in his corner, raised his muzzle and cocked his ears: a strangled groan came out of his throat. His master came over babbling tender phrases and coaxed him to sit back down, yet the dog continued to make dismal growls and bare his teeth.

"I hope he doesn't start barking right now," said Giuffrida. "He's never liked these noises very much."

The tape went back to an empty rustle; after a brief pause, a shallow crumbling noise took over, and beyond that I could just make out a hushed medley of voices. Every now and then a single voice would stick out from the choir, a metallic-sounding voice that seemed to express a clear desire to push its way through, to overtake the others stuck in their common effort. You sensed a rattling of boulders, like before a landslide; and soon a raucous cry burst forth while the pitter-patter chisel sounds grew furious. A second cry followed the first; then a third scream butted in; and each one of them oozed a sinister tone of triumph. It sounded like a messy geyser erupting, only the jets of steam rushing up from freshly opened craters were weirdly modulated murmurs, where a long "UUUUH" fell into a grating noise as if it were scratching the ground to gather stones and render them into a harsh "RRRRH," into a "CCCCH" pelting like a heavy rainstorm, into an exhausting "NNNNH": material stumbling blocks that allowed themselves to assimilate, it seemed, only after a distressing struggle. In between those rocky phonemes you could hear the faint hissing of an *S*, a dense smacking of labial consonants, and the thrashing rage of sounds that hadn't yet managed to escape from the deep. Gauguin scourged the air with his tail; his hair turned frizzy. At the first sign that he was going to bark, Giuffrida stopped the tape. He flung me an appraising glance as if hoping to gather my impressions, but since I was quiet and my poker face was impenetrable, he pressed "Play" again. What I'd just heard, he informed me, was the second phase of recordings, a remarkable in-between period spanning a week before the noises actually transformed themselves into words.

I noticed, as the tape's rustling resumed, that Giuffrida had bunged up his ears with his thumbs; I couldn't grasp the reasoning behind that gesture. I also noticed that the twitching of his face had intensified and that he was viewing the dog with obvious apprehension, though he didn't neglect to study me too, as if he expected some kind of reaction from me as I listened.

Right then, a sullen gurgle appeared without warning, a low agitation in gluggy waters, coming from a whirlpool. It began as a modest sucking noise, then, little by little, it spiraled into a ravenous, far-reaching withdrawal, as if hundreds of mouths were dipping into a monstrous water hole determined to tap it dry, as if a thousand-year-old thirst had finally found a wellspring where it could drink its fill. I was grabbed by a sickness that came from nowhere; it felt like those parched lips were inside me, siphoning away my lymph to slake their need. The malaise passed as quickly as it came, but now I too couldn't avoid clogging up my ears with my thumbs. Giuffrida noticed my problem and, with a prophetic smile, he stopped the tape a second time.

"All of this brings back memories, doesn't it?" he told me.

The suggestion was obvious and I found it redundant to answer him. The memory of Bergesio and his dried-up lake was still fresh in my mind. And in the time of mass insomnia, I too had suffered from a secret interior dryness, even though sleep had never completely forsaken me. Back then, I'd attributed my discomfort to the condition of my nerves worn out by an unpleasant day job, refusing to believe in the intervention of an external power: but now, hearing those whirlpools, my suspicion of having been at least partly the victim of a mysterious osmosis was making solid sense. Through which hidden pores did the slurry seep out into those lapping mouths? I looked at Giuffrida; he was pale. The wolf dog arose and paced around the room with his tail between his legs, whimpering. "Even he's a little bit depressed," said my host. "He's only five years old and he wasn't even born at the time of those recordings, but he's a sensitive animal and can't help but feel involved when he senses we're too close to danger."

"But ten years have come and gone now," I answered, hesitating, "and so the danger . . . should be gone too by now."

"It might still be here, endemic, latent . . . Of course, it suits us to believe that it's all in the past, but it would be brainless to give ourselves over to optimism. No one has ever ventured to make a detailed study of these facts; we prefer to smother them in a conspiracy of silence, denying the evidence too—fancy that! Now, in trying to lift the veil of *omertà*, there's a risk of colliding not only with those who are materially responsible for what happened, but those who consciously or unconsciously contributed to their outbreak of violence. It's not for nothing that, excluding myself, only you and Segre are aware of this cassette's existence."

"And the words? When do they appear?" I asked, feigning an interest that couldn't hide my nervousness.

"Now, listen. We should be clear on this: unlike those alleged 'voices' Raudive recorded, which typically expressed themselves in many different tongues and with bizarrely mangled words, the 'entities' I've captured on tape speak in Italian. That ought to be a sign that *we* were the ones who spawned these things; that it was our social—and I'll risk saying it, *urban*—environment that gave rise to them. If, one day or another, they appear in a different part of the world, then maybe we'll finally know . . . It would all depend on the habits and customs that govern public life in those hypothetical countries."

Quickly, Giuffrida wound the tape back and forth before stopping it at the part we were interested in, then let it run for a third time.

The voices didn't hesitate to make themselves heard. They spoke ponderously, as if every syllable were a dreadful burden to bear. When they fell silent, it sounded like a bag full of rubble had dropped. But you never heard them taking a single breath: the suggestion of fatigue came from the weight of the language. I couldn't even understand the meaning of the sentences, which evaded every rule of accent and punctuation: the pauses were a fixed occurrence, arising from the struggle to haul the words, and each pause was closed off with suction.

"I didn't believe they were really speaking," said Giuffrida. "In my view they were *thought waves*, telepathic messages my apparatus had managed to pick up at random. Up to a certain point, anyone who came across those entities wouldn't have noticed anything; he would've found the usual radio noise. Only at the end, before the messages stopped and gave way to other happenings, was there a genuine—and peculiar—acoustic occurrence which the human ear could detect. If you have a little patience, you'll hear it as well."

I pricked up my ears. Now and then, within that strained pageant of voices, I could detect a number of syllables that colluded to form words. And so I could piece together the word "TREE-TRUNK" and then the word "WA-ALL" . . . As I focused harder, I noticed that each noun was preempted by the phrase "I-SPY" . . . You'd hear things like "I-SPY-A-TREE-TRUNK," or "I-SPY-A-WALL." They were pure and simple observations, as if, at the pinnacle of their rock-tunneling, their fluid drainage, these entities had gotten to the surface only to find what was right in front of their eyes and describe it in brief jottings. Then one voice, more sullen than the others, completed the sentence, "I-SPY-A-PATH-BE-TWEEN-THE-HOU-SES." And another voice, equally monotonous, answered, "I-SPY-A-WAY-THROUGH-THE-BUSH-ES." Gradually, the exchanges of information became more flexible. The muck that was slurped up at every pause seemed to act as a lubricant. But the conversation was still short on adjectives. These were nothing more than rigid descriptions of anything that happened to fall in their field of view. And it was a blinkered view, an immovable view, which the viewer didn't seem capable of escaping. Yet, in the repetitiveness of the observations (they announced the presence of a doorway no less than six times) there was a mounting stress that gave each new sentence a rabid impetus. Little by little, the ferocity shown by those entities as they rose to the surface was changing into bitterness—a bitterness caused by the inability to reach even broader horizons. It struck me, however, that not all of these creatures suffered equally in their state of optical imprisonment. One of them had just reported seeing an open sky and hills in front of him, and in his description, less cursory than the others, there was an air of smugness. I deduced that the mood that drove those voices was subject to impulses that weren't alien to human nature. Indeed, after that last message, there came a sort of snarling silence, during which I could only hear a feeble voice that said, as if mulling things over: "WELL-I-CAN-SEE-ON-LY-A-SIN-GLE-COL-LUMN."

Giuffrida hadn't stopped observing me. Though it betrayed his nervousness, he still managed to form a friendly expression, a knowing smile that seemed to say: *You're starting to figure things out, huh?*

Thus far, I could only speculate broadly. The voices had given up a few slivers of truth, but overall, my view of the phenomenon wasn't exactly clear. Of course, I had started to rule out that these were the "voices of the dead" or, as Giuffrida first guessed, radio hams in the mood for a prank. But I still didn't see a connection between these events and the heart of my research. What did any of this have to do with the massacres?

In the series of tape-plays that followed, I noticed a curious enrichment of the language. Adjectives had emerged, sentences were expressed in more sophisticated syntax, and the anonymous statements, the short-lived spurts of vision, had been replaced by narratives that were at times highly imaginative—as if these entities were in competition among themselves over who could best describe the view in front of them. The creature that had spoken about hills and open sky was now overtaken by a new voice, which butted in to describe the spectacle of a garden filled with trees and flowers. This was met with a cry of rage. A third voice, delicate and suggestive, interrupted, then lingered to describe the beauty of an enchanted castle with its towering spires and fantastic maidens who stood by the windows stroking their long hair. "That's what I spy!" the voice concluded, in a cutting, almost superior, tone. The catalogue of seamy urban views had practically vanished. The odd introvert remained in the background who accused fate of shortchanging him with unsatisfactory surroundings: cracked walls damp with piss, atrocious rolling garage doors, garbage bins standing in corners of a yard. And in those voices there was a gloomy desire for vengeance, a deathly yearning to stretch out their thirst for liquid. I heard a voice that said: "I spy colossal camphor trees; and there are sugar palms which, when lacerated, furnish a sweet and inebriating liquor; and farther ahead I spy superb betel palms that buckle from the weight of their clusters of ripe nuts; and still farther than that I spy beautiful mangosteen plants, each as tall as a cherry tree, whose fruit, as big as oranges, are the tenderest and most delicious in all the world; and I spy areca palms with huge leaves and gambier vines and gutta-percha trees and caoutchouc vines . . ." I heard a sigh of regret, a long, "OOOOH!" like a disbelieving lament. "You're lying!" a voice shouted. "Well, come and see if you don't believe me!" Then a new, defiant voice took over: "And I spy an islet three hundred and fifty meters long, shaded by beautiful sago palms and durians, defended at its eastern tip by an old but still sturdy Dayak fort, built with planks and poles of teak, a wood as hard as iron which can sustain fire from a cannon of no small caliber . . ." "LIAR!" "I only report what I see!"

"Sounds like Kipling to me," I told Giuffrida.

"Myself, I'd say it's Salgari . . . *The Pirates of Malaysia*, perhaps?" he clarified with a trembling smile.

Now it seemed that the imagination of those creatures had hit the limit of their capabilities. One spoke yet about an endless ocean, about vessels navigating its horizon; then came a reference to some kind of Islamic paradise populated by houris in see-through veils . . . There was more metallic cursing, and then the visionary competition came to an exhausted halt. A long silence took over. I heard a hollow droning like you'd get by pressing a conch to your ear. Out of that lull, that resonant cavity, a voice arose—gritty, quarrelsome, in a timbre that was now more metallic than ever, which made me think of the scourging voice of General Bixio as Lieutenant Abba recalled it in his memoirs.

"I think I'll just take this 'tropical island' off your hands!"

"And I'll come and boot you out of your little fortress!"

"Boot me out? We'll be the judge of that!"

"Then see how long you last, whelp!"

A string of hasty challenges from more places seemed to unite into a singular, communal desire: unseating anyone who boasted about alluring panoramas from his scrap of paradise and taking his place. After that, the voices lingered in discussion on the best way to give substance to that threat. The tone was dry and precise now.

"I spy a few things moving in front of me that I can bring to smite you with!"

"They won't be moving much longer! There's not much life in them left to suck!"

"Using them as swords or maces sounds fine enough to me!"

"Affirmative! We'll have to check that they're good and solid first."

"No objections there!"

"We'll test them first against the sidewalks."

"*Whosoever useth the stone to kill shall himself as a stone be used . . .*"

"On that we can all agree!"

"Let's choose when to commence hostilities."

"July the second! And we'll clash only by night!"

"Challenge accepted! From July the second we shall do battle, and it shall be *our* battle!"

"Yes, we shall do battle! Challenge accepted!"

And then there was a scream. A terrible scream, followed by

more screams, which resounded like echoes. I'd lost all doubt that these were war cries and not just "telepathic messages," as perhaps I'd thought until now.

"It's the screams Segre the attorney heard!" I exclaimed, looking at Giuffrida.

"And they were recorded on the ninth of May, at two o'clock in the morning; the time matches up," he pointed out, and stopped the tape.

"So finally we have the evidence."

"Evidence we have to keep very well hidden."

"And why's that?"

"No one would enjoy hearing exactly how those entities regarded us."

"What you mean is . . . I can't talk about it . . . in my book?" I asked in a modest, deflated voice.

"For sure you can talk about it . . . But many people will wonder why you hadn't spoken about it ten years ago. Their awareness at the time wasn't very different from the present; I suppose you also must've seen those footprints in the asphalt, the flower beds . . . and the places they led back to if you followed them."

Yes, I'd seen them—and I'd seen other things too! And so I lowered my head in silence and bit my lip, as if Giuffrida's words had wounded me, stripped me of my mask.

"But now . . ." I stammered, "now we know what the motives were . . . We know the *why* behind those murders."

"Motives in our own image and likeness," said Giuffrida, ejecting the cassette from the player and slipping it into a pouch.

I was about to say something else, perhaps another try at self-justification, when I saw him suddenly freeze like he was listening out for something. I barely had enough time to ask, "What . . . ?" before he seized me by the wrist and made me stay quiet. Gauguin had hurled himself against the door, barking; he seemed ready to scrape it with his claws. Then, after reaching the height of his rage, he suddenly fell back, his tail low, as if he were informed by an invisible fear.

"Keep still!" Giuffrida commanded. "There must be someone in the garden . . . I don't know who it is; usually thieves are far too scared of the dog to think about visiting me."

Listening, I couldn't tell if Gauguin's barks might've alternated between anger and terror, like a basset hound in front of a cat on the defensive. Then he settled down; a long, drawn-out growl vanished into a whimper, and he went back to crouching. "I think it would be better if I accompanied you back to wherever you parked your car," said Giuffrida, noticing that I'd turned pale.

"Do you happen to own a gun?" I asked.

"I don't like firearms. Having Gauguin around is enough to defend us, if there's any need for that."

He put the dog on a leash and led him all the way to the door. I followed behind cautiously, waiting for him to take the first peek into the garden. "It doesn't look to me like anyone's there," he said, sounding relieved. "Maybe it was a fox, or a weasel . . ."

I went and saw for myself, but I spotted nothing in the moonlight but a few scattered shrubs, a small tree and the statue of Diana gleaming white in front of them. I asked Giuffrida why he kept the statue and he replied that he'd bought it because it cost next to nothing. It was carved by a craftsman specializing in graveyard sculptures, and a bit of kitsch didn't hurt the overall environment: a touch of bad taste to give more standing to the valuable works.

We reached the car. Giuffrida shook my hand, gently, as he'd done when I'd arrived. I noticed that Gauguin was trembling and looking anxious. I didn't linger to ask my host if we'd meet up again. I could guess his answer only too well: he was the one with the information, and any plans he had for it were entirely his decision. I thanked Giuffrida, gave the dog a quick pat and drove off down the hill.

A car was following me.

VIII.
THE HEADLINES

I'D GOTTEN A LETTER from Ballarin in Venice, sent shortly
after his return. Despite my friend's certainty that Turin now
held me in chains like Prometheus bound to his rock, I eagerly
considered his invitation to pack my bags and meet up with
him. Ballarin explained that, dead city for dead city, in the Most
Serene Republic the eyes and ears could at least have their fill,
even if Marghera stank to high heaven. My artistic sense had to
take certain perks into account, however ephemeral they were.
Why leave off a decision indefinitely when it would only bring me
advantages? This was all very kind coming from a friend. I replied
that, for now, my work at the company was the only thing I had
to survive on: if I ever saw a chance to get a job in his neck of the
woods, I would've sprung on it immediately. Of course, I omitted
the essentials; my recorder wasn't like his flute—a hippogriff that
could be ridden at will, taking off into the air!

And I knew this well, especially after I'd made my visit to

Giuffrida. Even the comforts of Bach's sarabands and certain ada-gios by Vivaldi and Albinoni—which for better or for worse I'd always been able to perform and find relative peace in—were now lost to me. Any beauty their musical phrases once had could no longer move me. They felt strange and hollow, as if my memory of the slurping noise I'd heard at Giuffrida's house were acting retrospectively to drain me of pleasure. I felt run-down and bit-ter: I placed my hands on the instrument without any certainty and breathed out foolishly like someone puffing into a blowgun. I even tried to set aside the classics and throw myself into a punk-ish mode with noisy items chosen out of my kitchenware. Yet the battering of saucepans with ladles, the furious grating rhythm of knives being whetted, only made my inner condition worse: there was an endless surfeit of anguish and desolation that I couldn't expel.

I had an ugly dream. I dreamed that a bunch of young archae-ologists digging around Volterra had discovered bas-reliefs reveal-ing that the great poet Virgil had actually been an ostrich. The sculptures dated back to the Augustan period. The anonymous artist depicted the poet in various positions: standing upright with his long neck almost vertical and his tiny head and beak animated by two eyes that shone with intelligence; in another panel, you saw him running through the Imperial Palace and flapping his wings, among Pretorian guards with their weapons on display. This was followed by a group scene: "AVGVSTVS IMPERATOR" . . . "QVINTVS HORATIVS FLACCVS" . . . "PVBLIVS VIRGILIVS MARO STRVTHIO-CAMELVS" . . . "PVBLIVS OVIDIVS NASO," and next to them certain palace advisors. These revelations had touched the whole world and strengthened the case of those who believe that a sublime soul can reside even in the body of an animal.

The dream cast a sinister light on my recorder; it made me think of the pipes played by the shepherds who chitchatted in Virgil's *Bucolics*. I broke the instrument in half and threw it out the window. My dream vision of bas-reliefs had me scared. I'd seen them passing in front of my eyes, barely a hand's-breadth away; then, just as close, they hid themselves inside me so I could no longer see them but *feel* them. Their presence within me prevented examining what lay behind them; they had become the lid of a sarcophagus where all my richness was stowed away. Yet someone could very well have dug an underground tunnel to come and sap me dry.

In this mood of hesitation and self-doubt, I left the house at eight in the morning to go to work. Sometime around six in the evening I went to the public library to peruse old newspapers in the archives, which spoke of events I would've paid a fortune to forget. "IS THIS STILL THE CITY OF GRAMSCI AND GOBETTI?" read a headline in *La Stampa*. And elsewhere: "AN ERUPTION OF VIOLENCE"—"WAVE OF SENSELESS FURY SWEEPS ACROSS TURIN"—"SITUATION NOW CRITICAL"— "A DISTRESSING MYSTERY" . . . These were newspaper articles from the middle of July, when it was no longer possible to talk about scattered crimes, albeit with certain features in common, but genuine barefaced massacres. "If we were still dealing with a few attacks, even the frightening ones which happened on Corso Stati Uniti and in Piazza Carlo Felice, we could at least think it was the work of a madman; and this might have brought us some relief, both for our faith in wider humanity and knowing it wasn't politically charged," a police functionary told the press. "But when, as in this case, the madness has a collective quality and implications that may be ideological . . ."

Meanwhile, the *Gazzetta del Popolo* reported, "The festive atmosphere of summer seems to have fled in the wake of these massacres, a nightmare which our city, already plagued by mass insomnia, cannot easily take its mind from. The shopping arcade of Galleria Subalpina is flooded with the sound of shuffling crowds . . . There is a register for signed condolences, guarded by four officers, with a large bow of black crepe pinned to the flag just above the table. People flock to add words of support to these mortuary records which, for lack of more white space, are taken to the Town Hall. Some children believe that those papers are where grown-ups write down their wish-list for the holidays. It's difficult—impossible, even—to explain to them what they're seeing."

In the retail areas, most of all in the clothing stores, business stagnated painfully: "The mannequins, young and beautiful, smile with plastic faces at a sad, shriveled crowd . . ." And then came a message from the President of the Republic: "The horrendous bloodbaths which have sown death throughout Turin, a city dear to us indeed, leave our nation appalled by their monstrous savagery, by their magnitude and by the brutish recklessness with which they are carried out. Somewhere in this tragic chain of terrorist acts, there's a link that must be broken at all costs to safeguard the life and freedom of our citizens. It is up to the forces of democratic order; it's up to the court authorities, before whom lie a number of complaints against the incitement of terrorist acts, to give the rule of law back to the sovereign people who demand it. It's up to all citizens to support the efforts of justice and the forces of democratic order in the defense of life against this murderous violence. To you, Mr. Prime Minister, and to you, the Honorable Minister of the Interior, I express my highest solidarity for the action this government is undertaking in order to clamp down relentlessly on these criminal acts fixed on upsetting the free and democratic direction of our country. I wish to pass on the most heartfelt of condolences, on behalf of the Republic and myself, to the families of the victims."

Public opinion called for the punishment of the culprits and whoever may have incited them. Even the Church authorities demanded it: they certainly didn't look kindly on the suspicion, which was then nastily spreading, that the killers were being unleashed at nighttime from the Little House of Divine Providence. Whoever they were, they had nothing to do with the unfortunate guests of the house, who were in fact fully conscientious creatures. If they were evil, it at least wasn't by nature, but from the instigation of deviant ideologies . . . And people would do well to throw aside their misgivings about the Library, one of the few benevolent institutions, if not the only one, born in the midst of a society that had lost nearly all its moral sense!

On July the sixteenth of that year, a thirty-six-year-old man named Antonio Mangiaferri was arrested by a police unit at his house, a ramshackle dwelling on Via Barbaroux. The charges against him were based on the testimony of a tram driver who had seen him in Piazza Cavour behaving in a way that left no doubts. His height measured at six feet and two inches. He had a patchy history of delinquency. He had drifted from one job to another, either out of restlessness or from being regularly fired due to his rebellious nature. He read pamphlets inciting subversion. He nursed ambitions of becoming an actor which he hadn't managed to fulfill, except some bit parts in minor films that circulated around the fringes.

Mangiaferri's arrest finally allowed editors to splash their front pages with an image of "the monster himself." And he truly was a monster, with his vacant look, his long chin, his prognathic jawbone, a scar on his right cheek, a deep horizontal furrow cutting across his face—and huge hands that could've played lawn bowls with watermelons.

Everyone agreed that the witness could be counted on as a sensible, trustworthy person and a man of few words. "Angelo has a heart of gold," his brother said. "If he went to the police, to the carabinieri, to report a thing like that, you can be absolutely sure of what he says. I can say personally that he's had a photographic memory since he was a kid. For years, we helped our parents who ran a dry cleaner's. Angelo always remembered absolutely everything: the customers' names, their addresses. There was never a risk he was wrong. He could recognize—*with one glance*—all the garments that got given in for dry cleaning. And if you don't believe me, go and ask my mother, Francesca Moroni; she's seventy-four years old and she lives with my sister . . ."

The foreign press, however, remained puzzled in the wake of the arrest and the political motivations that were pinned to the crimes. It didn't match the descriptions of the killings, however woolly, given by tourists who had passed through Turin. One could agree on the gigantism of the murderers (though not in every case: some killers were of almost normal stature). Yet their rage didn't seem to revolve solely around human beings. No, they didn't just grab passersby and throw them on the pavement or against trunks. After they'd slaughtered a few citizens in that fashion, they seized others, choosing them with care out of the crowd. Having accomplished what seemed like a selection process, they used them as human cudgels to bash *one another.* That's right! And they weren't dressed in tatty clothes like Mr. Mangi-aferri. Some tourists swore that they'd seen them in sweeping, low-hanging cloaks—full of flouncy pleats—which opened at the front, revealing torsos enclosed by narrow blousons with long rows of buttons. Their breeches often clung tight to their legs. The expressions on their faces were nearly always serious and pensive, even in the heat of combat, which saw the "duelists"— such we'll call them—begin by moving close to each other, taking their time to square off properly. Once the distance between them had narrowed to one short step, they raised their human clubs and bludgeoned one another, quietly but furiously. Yet why they did it, no one really understood . . .

In the face of such feverish accusations, our own press reacted with unanimous outrage. Our delegates to the European Parliament threatened to quit if this foreign smear campaign against a city rich with glorious traditions wasn't stopped at once. And when the insinuations continued—as, indeed, did the killings—our threats took a more concrete form. The most alarming example of which was our determination not to repay huge debts to the International Monetary Fund.

Now the overseas papers became newly cautious. In a gambit that carried a strong flavor of reconciliation, the famous psychoanalyst Jean Lescaut expounded a theory within the pages of *Le Monde* that might have appeared to form a sensible compromise. The insomnia of the Turinese—whose causes, nonetheless, he could just barely understand himself—had brought citizens to the extreme limits of bearable psychic tension. When those limits were crossed, that tension exploded like a stick of gelignite; human antagonisms were magnified a hundredfold, and this could enable forms of aggression that were unthinkable in a normal situation. Such cruelty would fall on the first passerby who came to hand, and who in turn could very well be an aggressor. This also explained the code of silence that shut the lips of witnesses: Who would have the nerve to testify against his neighbor, when the following night, or the night after that, he too might behave exactly like him? The outpourings of grief inside Galleria Subalpina were a way to exorcise the sense of guilt that each citizen harbored deep within.

This explanation served to calm the waters. Our relations

with other European countries went back, in a manner of speaking, to normal. As for Lescaut's theory of psychic tension, it wasn't held in high regard by the investigators: it lacked an ideological motive, and if studied with care, it ultimately suggested an underlying grievance that compelled and affected all citizens without discrimination. As a consequence, it was found preferable to keep Mangiaferri behind bars and track down any individuals near him who may have been accomplices. Notwithstanding the protests of certain radical groups, the law never came around to prosecuting the people who found themselves in jail. After four years locked up, Mangiaferri and others like him were freed when their terms of remand in custody expired. But the Twenty Days of Turin— which ended on July the twenty-second as suddenly as they had begun—were a distant event by now, an event that no one wished to recall.

IX.
THE MESSAGES

I COULD NO LONGER SHAKE the feeling that I was under scrutiny, not since the night of my encounter with Sister Clotilde. There was the issue of the mute phone calls: I was getting at least two of them a day now. And the car that had followed me as I drove back from Giuffrida's house: a red Simca with two people inside. (I failed to get a good look at their sexes.) They could've overtaken me very easily if they'd had the mind to (I was hardly cruising in a muscle car like theirs) but instead they chose to tailgate me with a determination I wasn't at all enjoying. As I got home and parked by the main door, I noticed the Simca had stopped at the Gran Madre di Dio Church. It lingered there as long as I gave no move of letting myself into the hallway. At that point, it took off abruptly: a squeal of tires, and it sped away toward Piazza Vittorio! I had other suspicions as well, but ones too fuzzy to describe.

Instead, I'll touch on a new situation I got entangled in as I got home one day, after spending some time on my research at the public library. In the gap under the door I found a letter addressed to me. The sender's name wasn't given; if I wanted to reply to the message, I would have to go to an unused postal box in the area around Dora Station and deposit my response there. Now I'll give you the gist of what the letter said:

Dear Sir,

For a long time now—months, perhaps even years, I hardly know!—I have been writing one letter every day to one person picked at random from an old telephone directory. Nobody has ever written back to me, but this hasn't stopped me from trying. I don't know how to explain this resistance to starting a dialogue: maybe someone doesn't think I have a style that's quite ornate enough, or they imagine I want to sneak into their life uninvited, to rub the ointment of my soul all over their trousers, so to speak. This is absolutely untrue! Besides, it isn't like I'm asking anything from anyone; I've been an insurance agent since I was a young man and I can support myself. But enough of this preliminary talk; let's get to the point: making a reciprocal acquaintance, starting a dialogue, which of course will need your reply in case you DO consider it . . . To start off with, I used to have a dog . . . But maybe hearing about my dog isn't something you'd be at all interested in, in which event I'll tell you about myself. I'm the most charming fellow you could meet in person; I'm smallish, perhaps, but not unsightly. I lead a modest but dignified existence, just like anyone else. One

evening after another, I climb up to my little apartment, and
sometimes it's quite an effort because I live on the eighth floor
and there's no longer a staircase or an elevator—not since a
little while ago. During the climb, as I cling to any handhold I
can find, I can hear the pelting of garbage coming from above
mixed with the voices of annoyed tenants, but I never hear
anything besides that. Once I've managed to reach the top, I
attentively read an old newspaper which I found one day in the
rubbish heap. After the reading, which entertains me more and
more each time, I take care to put the paper back in its place
and I suck for five minutes on my maraschino cherries . . . At
the stroke of midnight I return them almost intact in their glass
jar where every day I see the level of saliva has risen a little
higher than its previous position . . . I don't deny, Dear Sir,
that now and then I'd like some companion to bear witness
to my joy. There's the dog—that much is true—but that's a
matter I'm not authorized to discuss, at least not until I get
your kind permission . . . Do I have it, Sir? Can we count on
such a thing? I hope I have told you with the utmost candidness
all that a man can say, without failing in the restraint which
would be only appropriate for a relationship in letters with a
stranger. As I await your answer, which may well be the start
of an exchange of mutually interesting views, you have my most
distinguished compliments. Please deposit any possible replies
in . . . [His instructions followed.]

Yours Most Truly,

At first it was easy to think this was a joke by a friend. But the surety that there was no one in my circle of colleagues who'd be inclined to such dark humor left me with a hunch that the business wasn't frivolous. The letter had a roundaboutness that came a bit too naturally. Even the place it indicated where I was supposed to deliver my answer was in keeping with its contents. Whoever it was who'd appeared anonymously to slide the letter under my door, I didn't think the other occupants of the building had any hand in it. And indeed I knew all of them: quiet unobtrusive people, lacking all irony, comfortable in their sturdy family attachments. Yes, sirree! The only one who had what we might call a "personal motive" for behaving in that way, was *me*! But come now! Surely I was still some way away from developing a split personality! In any case, I put the letter aside, promising to get back to it later with a cooler head. The day's surprise had taken away my appetite. I left off the preparations for my solitary dinner to a later hour. What's more, I'd come down with a headache; and what better cure for that than a nice walk around the neighborhood? It was a peaceful night; a spring breeze was rolling through that made the perfect painkiller for my aching cranium. I took a few deep breaths (expanding my abdomen, as the yogis teach, in order for oxygen to reach the base of the lungs). It was around half-past eight: an hour when the city crowds start thinning out of deference to household rites, and the bars enjoy a few moments of respite waiting for an invasion of patrons who won't arrive a minute before nine. This was the upper limit of silence that I could hope to get if I wanted the pain that was crushing my head to loosen its grip.

I gazed at the sky and noticed that the moon was waning. A neon sign on the other side of the street was faulty. On my own side, there were three cars parked in single file along the sidewalk, all with the same make, color and model; even their license plates had certain numbers in common. It seemed to me that there were fewer pedestrians around than usual. On my right side—I still hadn't set off toward the bridge crossing the Po as I'd intended to do—two young men with neat blond hair, wearing dark suits and purple ties, were talking to each other. Now and then they shot me sideward glances. They looked like a pair of Mormons; I'd seen similar types canvassing for their sect in front of Porta Nuova Station—their cheeks rosy, their necks eternally clean-shaven.

As soon as they saw me staring at them, they bolted, vanishing behind the nearest corner. Among the cars that were parked across the street, I noticed a red Simca, which for some reason I came to associate with the youngsters. There was no evidence to suggest that they were harboring any particular designs: until a short time later, when I saw them reemerging to my left—having, it seems, just skirted around the block—and making for the Gran Madre di Dio Church. They stopped under the main steps and gawked at the stone statues for some time. I wondered if they might've had something to do with the Millenarists. I recalled, however, that the Millenarists tended to dress on the casual side and their attitude was fairly laid-back. But these young men had a severity about them that left you anxious. That, I could tell you very well, because, seeing that they weren't moving from their position, but rather stood there nailed to the spot in front of one of the neoclassical statues that kept guard over the steps, I carefully brought myself closer to snoop at what they were doing. One of them was holding a walkie-talkie and whispering something I couldn't catch. Both of them glared at the statue with tenacity, almost as if they were expecting a response. Even I joined them in staring at it from my hiding place: I wouldn't have been shocked if the sculpture suddenly gave an approving nod. But since—to my huge relief—nothing happened, I left them and got back to my stroll.

I spent half an hour wandering through the arcades of Via Po, pausing to look at shop windows. On the way back, I noticed that the two youngsters were gone, and there was no more of the Simca either. So there *was* something to my suspicions after all! I couldn't rule out a relationship between these two characters and the car that had followed me down the hill. I went to take another look at the statue. While I was studying its Olympic indifference, I glimpsed, through the corner of my eye, a white figure at the top of the steps. I sprang around. The church's entrance had one door wide open, and, against the darkness within, what I saw was almost wraithlike. She was gazing at me forcefully with her arms crossed over her chest, and in her eyes there was an inquisitorial determination . . . "Sister Clotilde!" I stammered. I fully expected she would come to meet me and rebuke me for not obeying her and her sisters' exhortations . . . The distance between us didn't allow me to take in the expression on her face and my imagination began to play tricks: now it seemed deadly serious; a moment later I swore she was laughing. Was her white habit moving in the breeze, or were the folds as stiff as marble?

I couldn't bear the ambiguous sight any longer. I started hiking up the great steps, but my feet didn't get very far before she turned away and disappeared into the church. The door closed gently, without a sound.

There was nothing I wanted now except to flee the scene, get safely home and bolt the door. I switched the radio on at full blast; then I prepared my dinner with unusual diligence; I even consulted a recipe book I'd inherited from my mother. After I'd eaten and turned the volume down, I sat at my desk and reread the anonymous letter. Well, I had to do something to keep my mind busy! I couldn't count the recorder among my personal belongings anymore, having roundly destroyed it. So I tried jotting down a few sentences. I can't remember what I wrote, just that I slipped the letter in an envelope; the following day—it hurts me to admit this—I went and deposited it near Dora Station, exactly as my pen pal had asked.

One afternoon, coming home from the office, I found a second letter under my door:

Dear Sir,

I have received your letter which is, overall, most interesting.
In fact, I had to carry it in my mouth so my hands could
remain free, since my building's Administration still hasn't

provided a more reasonable way to climb back up into my apartment . . . But all things considered, there's no harm in a bit of exercise—especially with the atmosphere these days, oh, the atmosphere! You'll excuse me, Dear Sir, if I respond to you without having read the whole of your letter yet, but a thorough reading isn't something one can do on the spot. On the other hand, maybe this isn't actually true: maybe I read it, but for some reason it said nothing to me (for instance, the lighting is totally inadequate within these premises) . . . But now we're talking about something else. I would like to provide you, Dear Sir, with an image of the tenement I live in. My building is a very high cylindrical tower. A long time ago, the stairwell was demolished. The Administration at the top floor has issued a memorandum in which it explained the reasons for this decision, but that's not the most important thing. (When there's a wall, there's a way! A way to climb it, I mean.) What leaves me baffled is that the Administration has begun to use the stairwell shaft as a garbage dump. At first I didn't take much notice: it was old furniture, books, papers, kitchen scraps. But later, the nature of the waste started to become—how to put this?—somewhat more challenging and personal. One would find—if you'll permit me the term—human excrement, which fell from above in ever increasing amounts. Over several years, the level has risen to the point that it now reaches the first floor of units, where mercifully only the working families live. And all of this has happened without a word of explanation! More than that, the fear of even stricter sanctions is so great

that the other tenants are silent, as if being covered in s*** by
the powers of the gerontocracy (up above, they're all old) was
perfectly normal. Now, Dear Sir, I ask you . . . Does all of that
seem reasonable? Does it seem fair? I'm sure you'll answer
me . . . And so then, Distinguished Sir, as I await your letter,
which will be one of the most cherished gifts I could ever hope to
receive, you have my very best wishes,

Yours Most Truly,

The fact that I'd succumbed to the temptation of replying
to this stranger left me feeling a profound despair. I didn't know
how to match this failure of mine to any desire aside from a wish
to alleviate the endless grind of my research. It was as if I'd been
working to flush out an enemy and getting into bed with him at
the same time. Of course, every day I was going to either the Civic
or the National Library, and on each occasion I'd make some little discovery. One Saturday morning, I went to a barbershop in
Piazza Lagrange (Eligio's, for those who don't know the place),
not so much to get a shave, but to chat with the owner a bit. I
imagined that he possibly had some useful information to share.
He'd been running his shop in the piazza for twenty years and he
must've seen a few things around that area!

As Eligio got ready to give my head the scissor treatment, I
opened the latest issue of *Tuttosport*; I thought I could use it to
start up a conversation, and indeed it wasn't long before the sub-

ject of football had helped break the ice between us. It was easy enough to gather which team he supported, and I didn't fail to make it known that it was my team too. I left it up to him to go into the details about this or that player's style on the field, and, showing that I always agreed with him, just as his harshest critic died down, I told Eligio that he could count himself a lucky man. Not only would his team win the championship this year, but he also had the satisfaction of working in one of the loveliest little squares in Turin. I didn't know what I would've given to be in his place! I described how squalid the street was where I worked at my day job, and how dull my white-collar duties were—certainly not worth the effort of a university degree! Eligio said I was utterly right. His parents had wanted to send him off to university but he held his own: he'd be a barber or he'd be nothing! In that, he'd succeeded, and now he was more than pleased with himself.

"This square . . ." I began casually. "At one time it used to be called 'Piazza Paleocapa'? Wasn't that the name?"

Eligio pretended he hadn't heard me.

"I'm asking because I came by here once—it must've been quite a while ago—and it seemed to me that on that pedestal there was a monument to Pietro Paleocapa—you know, the engineer and government minister—not to Lagrange."

"Oh, yes?"

"It might be because I don't often visit the center of town," I insisted, "and I don't follow too closely how things are going at your end, but I could swear the name of the square used to be different . . . Have you been in this spot for long?"

"About nineteen years now."

"Then you must've noticed the change . . . And you've never wondered why?"

"I normally just do my job and don't take notice of what's going on outside," Eligio said, hurrying the movement of the scissors. "And when the mayor changed the statues around, I was up in the mountains."

"Why do you suppose it was the mayor who changed them around?"

"Who else could it have been? If you want to see the monument to Pietro Paleocapa, you only have to cross Piazza Carlo Felice and you'll find it on the other side . . . Anyway, the statues are perfectly fine where they are, just as I'm perfectly fine *right here* . . . Do you want me to take some more off the sides?"

"No, thanks, keep the trim low."

A customer had come in, a cockeyed, brawny type. He had grabbed a magazine and started to leaf through it noisily. In the mirror I could see that he was relentlessly shifting his legs from position to position.

"You're a proper Turinese?" I asked Eligio. "From the central city?"

"Well, I was born here, if that's enough."

"Then it follows that there must've been other changeovers like this one?"

The customer had lowered his glossy reading and Eligio turned to look at him; I thought I saw the two of them exchanging a wink.

"You mean to say . . . ?"

"Yes, I mean other names that have—somehow, somewhere—been swapped around."

"No . . . None that I'm aware of . . . I'm not even sure, really . . ."

"So just here? Lagrange sitting in place of Paleocapa, and Paleocapa instead of Lagrange . . . It seems like those two weren't very happy with the spots they had before."

"So? Are *you* happy in the spot you're sitting?" Eligio replied, with heavy sarcasm.

"Well, things could be better, to be honest."

The customer had started to chuckle; I felt obliged to follow his lead.

"As you can see, we each have to make do as best we can . . . Even I would like to be working in Piazza San Carlo, maybe, or running a fancy-schmancy salon for the ladies . . ."

I couldn't blame Eligio for that; but the chuckles of the customer, which sounded cruder and more grating by the minute, incited me to press on.

"Yes, I agree with you that few people are happy where they sit . . . But if they all tried to change places with others who were better off—or rather, others whom *they imagined* were better off—they would have to carry out so much bloodshed that, as a result, only a couple of people out of every thousand would find their position transformed . . . Well, I think it's better to leave everything where it is."

There was an onerous silence. The client stopped laughing and took cover behind his glossy weekly. Eligio put down the scissors and grabbed the razor. Suddenly I felt a sharp prickling at my right cheek. "Ouch!" But Eligio was ready to block my hand from rising . . . "Don't touch it!" he said. "It's nothing! I'll disinfect it with alcohol . . ."

I allowed him to fetch a cotton ball to press onto the cut. It didn't take much for me to realize Eligio didn't like my choice of subjects. I reopened the *Tuttosport* and tried to read it once more. When I raised my eyes again I noticed that the customer was gone . . . Eligio pretended not to notice my surprise. He asked me to take off my glasses because he had to run the razor against my sideburns. I obeyed in silence. We didn't exchange any more words. After he'd finished combing me, he asked if I wanted some cologne. I told him I was fine. He went to get the mirror and show me the finished haircut. It was decent enough. Eligio brushed my shoulders and handed me an exorbitant price. I paid him and went out into the square . . . The monument to Joseph-Louis Lagrange looked a bit out of sorts on that pedestal; the inscription didn't match up to his biography as a mathematician. If Lagrange had ever been a "hydraulic engineer and eminent statesman," it was certainly news to my ears. I thought that if I were a sculptor I would have made some corrections to the monument . . . Yet I had to admit that I felt a touch out of place myself, even if I didn't know enough to say what my rightful condition could be.

X.
NEW GLEANINGS

I KEPT UP MY CORRESPONDENCE with the stranger, but it's probably useless for me to linger on the content of our letters. All I can say is that I made an attempt to pick out my mystery pen pal—a nocturnal ambush, close to the spot where I'd deposited one of my envelopes. I was left waiting well after midnight but, perhaps because of the rain or for some other reason, I saw no trace of him. That didn't prevent another of his letters from reaching my home, this time sent by regular mail.

To interrupt our exchange of letters—at least from my end—came a series of small incidents that I took note of walking around the city. I'll try to explain as broadly as I can. Indeed, it took me quite some time myself to grasp that these events had, so to speak, an abnormal character. Who would pay attention to an individual who stops for a moment at a public wastebasket—one bin out of the many standing around—to throw in an advert or a leaflet? Or a man or woman who bends down to pick something off the ground, just like a hobo gleaning a used cigarette? It would take the trained eye of a film director to notice such things. And even then, why would they do it? To shoot a documentary about urban life? How much of it would be worth recording?

If I came to realize an unnatural side to the whole affair, I owe it entirely to my mail-drop intrigue with the stranger. His words had left my eyes rather sensitive to everything involving dross or waste . . . And so it struck me that not everyone was using those bins to *get rid* of wastepaper they didn't need; some of them were putting their hands inside to *take things out*, then hiding whatever they'd taken deep in their pockets. Even the people who bent down on the pavement seemed to have a very special interest in the paper refuse: they weren't just grabbing coins, lost stamps, packs of smokes that might've still had a cigarette inside—at least not all of them were.

Hence I too started rummaging around in those receptacles, collecting balls of scrunched-up paper seeded throughout the streets.

For the first few days, I didn't land on anything remarkable. But one morning—as I traveled to work on foot, for a change—I found something in my hands that put me on the alert. It was a small notebook, the kind you can buy at a tobacconist's, with rather messy binding and greasy sheets of squared paper filled top to bottom with minuscule handwriting. There was a date on each page and the last page had a name and address. I started reading it, and at once I could tell what it was. I'd found a diary! A diary very similar to the ones that were donated ten years before to the now-defunct Library! Similar by general kinship . . . Its content went well beyond the typical confessions of before: here, we had signs of a dreadful aggravation! I shoved it back into the bin I'd taken it from, then, at the cost of being penalized for turning up late for work, I stopped and kept my eye on the opposite sidewalk. It didn't leave me disappointed. After an hour or so— during which many citizens had surrendered their litter to the bins out of pure civic duty—I saw a person approaching the container with something voracious in his stare. He was a man just about my age, a still-respectable period of his life. He could well have been a fellow tenant at the house I lived in. But the way he plunged his hands into the bin, how he wormed around inside it, and the gleam of perverse joy that appeared in his eyes as soon as he had extracted a notebook, made for very telling signs. He gave it a greedy look and pocketed it, then walked away in haste, keeping close to the walls.

I'm not going to pause, then, to enlarge on the reasons why I cut short my correspondence with the stranger. The vision of that solitary passerby had unsettled me all the way to my marrow. I realized, what's more, that I wasn't the only one studying the sidewalk: at the opposite corner of the same block, I noticed two other people who'd also found it extremely riveting to follow that sequence of events. Except that, while I was horrified, they seemed pleased with the outcome. They jotted down observations on a little notepad, exchanged wily glances every so often and gave knowing smiles. Both of them were young, refined-looking people that any respectable family would be delighted to invite over for dinner. They wore dark suits like those fellows I saw in front of Gran Madre de Dio. They made me think of the kids ten years earlier who'd been set loose to canvass for the Library at people's doorsteps; only there was no contagious enthusiasm in these youngsters, just a cold determination to achieve a goal that was unclear to me . . . Shortly afterward they were approached by a third figure—somewhat older, with chunky, black-rimmed glasses—and left the notepad in his hands. He nodded at the pair, who departed in different directions. When I set off for work again, I had to call on all of my willpower not to look behind me: if I'd noticed someone following me at that moment, I wouldn't have had the wits for simple arithmetic, let alone my day job!

At work, I was summoned by the company director, who upbraided me for being late too many times. I promised to be more punctual. He gave me a letter that had reached him, and said that the envelope, addressed to me, had come inside another envelope bearing his own name. He couldn't explain to me why it had happened; still, I swore I'd warn my friends that my boss didn't fancy being viewed as my postman. On their behalf, I felt the need to apologize. I pocketed the envelope and went to my cubicle.

Before I got started on another day of form-filling, I decided to read the letter. It was the stranger. I sensed he would be sending me letters through the director from now on—and, of course, explaining his motives for doing so at painstaking length. He brought me news of a personal nature: the filth had reached the sixth story; two more floors now and it would be touching him. He'd have to spend the remainder of his days under house arrest. However, he hadn't ruled out being able to live to the age of ninety. In fact, he had begun to consider the possibility of surviving on human excrement—and that, while the tenants on the ninth floor (very old, but as eternal as the whole Administration) were uncorking champagne bottles and munching caviar! The fact didn't seem quite as unfair to him now as it had once been: it was rather in harmony with the laws of Creation. He hastened to write this. Within two weeks' time, it would be physically impossible to continue our correspondence. This time, however, I didn't reply to him. Leaving the office—and perhaps I shouldn't have done this—I threw the stranger's letter into the wastepaper bin where I'd found the notebook, adding another "addressee" to the mix. Maybe somebody plucked it out and took my place as pen pal. I didn't stay to keep watch; there were already "others" around quite happy to shoulder that task.

ⓔⓧⓓ

In the middle of the night, I was woken with a start by a terrifying blow against my front door; I struggled to fall asleep again—was this how the insomnia began?—and the terror I felt at the blow echoing in the stairwell mingled with my anger at the surprise awakening. I wanted to run downstairs in my pajamas to teach a lesson to whoever had disturbed my rest, but I stayed tucked in. There was too much violence in the impact; it couldn't have been produced by a human fist, not unless it came equipped with a hammer—but not even that! If anything, it had to be a mace, like the ones medieval warriors used. My fear kept me from even looking out the window. I had the suspicion that this was just what the "mace-bearer" was waiting for: to see my head stick out so he could strike me on the forehead with another blow. I took three sleeping pills and decided to leave off examining any damage to the door until daybreak.

But early in the morning—before my alarm was timed to ring—the phone set out to inflict another shock to my already insecure sleep. This, however, wasn't another mute caller; it was Segre the attorney, and he was panting heavily. He apologized for waking me so early in the morning but a dreadful thing had happened that he'd only discovered now. The newspapers hadn't even mentioned it in the obituary columns . . . The event dated back to a few days ago. He felt obliged to warn me as soon as he'd gotten the impression that we were both in danger. Perhaps we'd do well if we could get together soon, preferably that evening. Paolo Giuffrida had been murdered! He'd been found dead in his garden, strangled, as if someone had placed two thumbs on his windpipe and throttled him. Gauguin was left for two days, trembling and howling against an iron railing, until a dogcatcher came and put him down with a strychnine shot. Segre had no doubt that they'd stolen Giuffrida's cassette of "voices"; as for the physical perpetrator of the killing, he preferred not to give me his ideas over the phone. Hiding behind the crime, Segre believed, there must have been something even more worrying . . .

I took a moment to get dressed and jump in the car. Not caring again whether I was late for work, I drove up the hill to reach Giuffrida's home. I wanted to check what had happened with my own eyes. I didn't manage to see very much, however: the house was cordoned off by police, who asked me what reasons I had just for trying to get near the gate. I said that I was a friend of the victim and that I'd only recently learned of his death; I asked when the funeral was set to be held. "No funeral!" an officer shot back. I took a glance at the garden through the railing: everything looked calm and ordinary. If the authorities were searching the house, they were doing it discreetly; the front door was closed. I saw the statue of Diana the Huntress, still there, secure on her pedestal; there were no signs of footsteps around her; no ground had been disturbed. Tidy flower beds, tidy pebbles: everything seemed like it was recently raked. If it hadn't been for the presence of the police I would've sworn that Giuffrida was still alive and that Segre the attorney had invented the news . . . Failing to worm anything out from the surroundings, I left soon enough. That evening, toward nine o'clock, I met Segre in Piazza Castello.

He wore a pale leather jacket, dark brown velvet trousers, a blue shirt and a flamboyant print necktie in perfect balance with the rest. Remembering his phone call, I'd expected to see him arrive looking ragged like me, and I felt a bit ashamed for letting myself be carried away by emotion at the cost of decorum. He almost appeared to be smiling; when he invited me to come with him into a typical piazza restaurant, where patrons sat exposed to the street through a glass window, I asked him if it mightn't be better to go somewhere more private for our dinner. He replied that it made no difference. Someone who truly wanted to shadow us would find a way—even if we chatted underground in one of the sapper tunnels Pietro Micca dug at the Siege of Turin!

At the table, I consulted the menu very carefully, lingering especially on the wines, and after Segre had agreed with me on a light wine from the Cinque Terre region that seemed first-rate, he gave a nod to the waiter. He made some choices from the menu that I didn't object to, then came to our main topic. His opinion was that I had to leave the city. It didn't matter where I went; the important thing was that I didn't stay in Turin, at least not for the time being. The problem wasn't as serious for him: he would leave for England the following day; he had a busy work schedule that would keep him away for quite some time, and being a man of the law, he could always watch his own back— even now. I mentioned Venice to him . . . Yes, he knew someone in Venice who could point me toward a job. If I needed some money to quietly leave town, he was happy to lend it without a due date for the repayment . . . In the end, he felt a little bit responsible for my fate: he was the one who'd sent me to Giuffrida; if I hadn't gone to listen to the tape with the "voices," my situation would be quite different, and maybe, who knew, Giuffrida might still be alive.

"And why on earth is that?" I asked, fearful.

"Because Giuffrida and I were the only ones who knew about the 'voices'; when they realized that we'd introduced a third party—and many were already aware of your research—they began to sense the danger that the knowledge would spread, and there's someone who absolutely cannot allow you to publicize it.

"And who is that 'someone'? The regional authorities? The mayor?"

"Mayor Bonfante is one of the most honest and decent people I know. It's not the forces that he represents which you should be worried about . . . It's something very different, with a history that goes quite a ways back . . ."

I filled my glass up to the brim.

"Have you sensed anything odd these past few days?" I asked him.

I told Segre everything that had happened to me, starting from my encounter with Sister Clotilde.

"I see . . . The envelopes from your mystery pen pal, the people picking manuscripts up off the streets, those polished-looking young men with their walkie-talkies in front of the statue at Gran Madre de Dio, the loud blow struck against your door last night . . . A business which we believed was over and done with is coming back into motion, and with a coldness, a clarity, which would have been unthinkable in the time of the Twenty Days . . . Perhaps even the letters you'd gotten from that stranger were part of the design."

"In what sense?"

"I think they might've been a lure, an attempt to snare your subconscious mind and reduce it to passivity. Whoever wrote them knew his addressee very well, weaknesses and all . . . Too many things about us are already on record . . . They wanted to pry open a chink in your armor and use your determination to their own advantage . . . With you, they only got midway, but who knows how many more gullible people have fallen into their trap? . . . They even tried to do it with me."

"If that's the case," I postulated, "then we shouldn't have any reason to fear for our lives . . . The trap hasn't sprung; our energy is still there, for the most part."

Segre looked at me, smiling at my naïveté.

"If they haven't taken the vim out of you," he said, "it's because, in some way or another, you put up resistance . . . And the hidden power that's being marshaled is *not amused* by people who resist. In the era of the Library, the followers of that power sought above all to splinter our will, to push us all the way to rock-bottom. The results went far beyond their expectations and many of them must have remained astonished; but certain events, once they're called forth, even unconsciously, might be irreversible. Or maybe those powers are reviving because they've come across the nourishment they need once again: you can always find people willing to offer it. The murderers from the Twenty Days no longer seem like the absolute protagonists under the new situation; they're only pawns, by the looks of it. It seems like mysterious fellowships have been formed . . . A violence that's less tumultuous, more selective and purposeful, but no less dangerous for that reason . . ."

I felt Segre was coming to a very delicate point; I wanted to ask him why these instruments of death and their allies or instigators couldn't in the end be fought, exposed to public opinion . . .

"I don't think we can establish any trail of concrete evidence joining those murderers with whomever—at least to our appearance—happens to command them. The evil is too deep-rooted, yet also too widely sown, entangling people, objects and objectives . . . The physical executors of its crimes are entities much too far beyond suspicion, since one cannot even mention them without feeling reason crumbling. Absolute evil couldn't have taken a more unassailable form . . ." Segre eyed me severely. "I fear today that if the two of us were bold enough to come clean about our speculations, we'd have a hard time managing to express ourselves except in deep allusions. Even the foreign papers, ten years ago, never went far enough to call them by name: they digressed in describing the massacres, they wrapped them up with words, but who dared to ever say what they really were? That duty far exceeds our simple capabilities . . . So I wonder if *you* might dare to tell me, right now, as plainly as you can: Who are the murderers?"

He pointed a finger at me and began dinging his plate with a fork. And when I couldn't respond, he said, "See now if I'm right or not? I too wouldn't risk it . . . It would be too humiliating to admit the evidence, declaring that something emerged from *nowhere at all* to capitalize on our 'power vacuum.' I'm no scientist, but I think a biologist, a physicist, an expert in mineralogy—none of them would know enough to make a diagnosis of such phenomena, not without taking that 'power vacuum' into account."

"And yet . . . the evidence was there . . . And it would still be there if . . . if we wanted to hold people to their responsibilities," I said, now in the grip of despair, knowing well that I was mangling my words.

"The evidence! And you think anyone cares about the evidence? . . . Perhaps you're alluding to the imprints on the flower beds, on the asphalt, to photographs that were taken and which nothing has been heard of since? To certain ludicrous nocturnal pursuits, carried out by the forces of justice, which ended as soon as the murderers returned, motionless, to the places they came from? There was no lack of evidence, that's for sure! But if nothing came out of it, perhaps we should look elsewhere for the reasons why . . . Even Nature can become depraved if people relentlessly incite it to do so . . . And Nature must have had an interest, taking an unscrupulous glance at our history where it discovered the perfect setting it needed to try out some new experimental form of life. Those who are unmoving, those who are beyond suspicion—as far as they are inert and familiar—and yet soaked in blood from head to toe, have always found ideal living conditions and absolute safety in our country. Millions of mouths have always protected them, whether screaming their praises or staying firmly zipped. Understanding this, Nature may have decided to go one step further, which was impossible until now. Can you point to anything more permanent, anything harder to suspect, than those murderers?" added Segre with an ironic touch, topping up his glass and mine. "Or instead of answering, wouldn't you rather drink up?"

I followed his second suggestion. The giddiness that the wine gave me sat well enough with my tablemate's dizzy dialectic. I began to drink without restraint.

"But why . . . here, exactly . . . in Turin?"

"Bah . . . Who knows? Perhaps because we're an isolated city, out of the international time stream, where certain experiments can be carried out without drawing too much attention . . . What do *we* know about what's going on in remote planets, which our telescopes and probes can never dream of reaching? These 'security concerns' have prompted Nature to select Turin out of all cities!"

"So what do we do now?" I said, covering my face with my hands.

"Do you still want to write your book on the Twenty Days?" Segre asked enigmatically.

I shook my head.

"Right, then! There's nothing left to do but get ourselves out of danger . . . Even if we'd never presume to sound the names of the killers, telling who it was who strangled poor Giuffrida, it's likely others will still believe we're able to do it. Their 'security concerns,' unfortunately, don't play in our favor: the perverse scheme that's unfolding is ready to do anything not to be hindered . . . As for the government authorities and the mayor, I fear they couldn't be much help. Bonfante's too much of a quibbler, and the establishment was always too cautious when it was necessary to intervene, before the evil outgrew measurement on a human scale . . . Our chances of recuperating, over time, have shrunk to but a small glimmer of hope . . . It's very hard to rebuild anything when you haven't yet severed the serpent's head."

Segre began to peer into his wine glass, like an oracle scrutinizing a crystal ball. "The future is very dark . . . Foul, small-minded deities have emerged from the heart of the rock . . . And beings of flesh and blood, like us, are celebrating this atrocious event . . . Promise me you'll leave the city?"

"Yes, I'll promise you that."

"And to do it as fast as you can?"

I promised him that as well.

"Now we can try to finish our meal."

I thanked him again for his offer to lend me money, but I had some savings and there'd be more from my severance pay. Segre gave me the address of a Venetian friend of his and said he'd write to him to pre-announce my arrival. Leaving the restaurant, he parted with a friendly, melancholy smile. When I arrived home, a bit shaky from too much wine, I examined my door. It hadn't taken a bang from anyone's mace . . . What I saw was the imprint of a hand!

XI.
TAKING LEAVE

WHY NOT JUST TELL you the truth? I was starting to feel happy. Maybe Segre's theories didn't seem so ridiculous the next day when I could view them with a clear head. Maybe we truly had hit rock-bottom. When you find yourself staring at unavoidable disaster, at the "point of no return," the idea of escaping it feels like the perfect medicine. And here my hide was at stake! So I won't get into detail about my preparations for departure, my resignation letter to the boss, the send-offs and best wishes from my colleagues, nor the process of booking a seat on the plane for that weekend—destination: Venice. I'll only emphasize one detail, my purchase of a new recorder. I posted a letter by express to Ballarin telling him about my arrival and (with him firm in my mind) about the instrument, which to me now held a symbolic meaning: my honest intention to draw closer again to that "largesse of spirit" from which, perhaps mistakenly,

I felt rejected. The Twenty Days could go to hell, and my research with them! What I needed now was inner peace!

I now had very little time left to pay my farewells to Turin, and I spent it by traipsing far and wide across the city, in a manner almost caressing it. There was no longer any reason to fear my enemies, who by this stage were surely well updated on my plans . . . When someone's already in a scramble to "get out of the game," why waste effort making sure his lips stay sealed? Yes, indeed, I spotted a few of *them* around, patrolling the streets with their dark suits, their notepads for jotting observations, their walkie-talkies. It hardly took much insight to know that a new "hidden power" was preparing itself, that the Library was getting back on its feet vigorously enough, albeit in new shapes and guises. The insomnia made its comeback, save that the victims were no longer being seized as clubs by unmentionable entities battling among themselves. Now they were left to waste away until they dried out completely, and then—who knew?— perhaps someone saw to making them disappear, like abductees, removed from sight.

I wanted to spend my remaining time in the outer neighborhoods. Mayor Bonfante and his council were hard at work: I found greenery zones where years before there had only been concrete and asphalt . . . quite a few women's clinics . . . The Rest Home for the Aging Poor no longer seemed like the waiting room for a cemetery; now it was an oasis of bliss where I wouldn't have scorned to spend my last days . . . And there were so many kindergartens!

One evening, after dinner, I paid a visit to the neighborhood of Pietra Alta. I'd always been impressed, whenever I'd driven along Corso Giulio Cesare to reach the expressway, by the presence, to my left, of a church shaped like the prow of a ship: a fairly modern red-brick building with a grayish front entrance. A strange temple this was, built—following an image in the Gospel of Matthew—to symbolize the unshakable voyage of the Church through the centuries. Before I left, I wanted to finally see that neighborhood up close. I came there shortly after ten o'clock, on the eve of my departure. I found the atmosphere a little disheartening . . . Maybe it was because of the church, which was much taller than I'd imagined; it looked more like an icebreaker than a cruise ship: an icebreaker of which nothing remained but the bow, yet so immense that its circumference outdid all of its counterparts in the Atlantic. And the neighborhood mood was tense. Even in a large courtyard where some youths were having a volleyball match, there was no playfulness. The yard lay at one side of the church, below the level of the road, isolated by a high chain-link fence. THE KIDS' REPUBLIC, one read on a banner.

It occurred to me that I was the only person watching the game. Everyone else threw shifty glances at the players, not siding with either team on the field, and dragged themselves along the sidewalk, their faces sad and worried. It seemed less like a sporting event and more like an occupation of territory. In fact, those kids wearing dark tights (there were girls as well), all with well-brushed short hair, were utterly silent except for the thudding of their hands against the ball. They didn't seem to care which way the match went; it was as if they were in the courtyard purely to send the message: *Look out, we're here!*

I asked a passerby what the name of the church was, and he told me it was called Our Lady of the Straight-and-Narrow Path. I went into a bar to have a coffee, then proceeded on to the neighborhood streets. I was fascinated by the effect the church gave when seen from the front; I paused in Via Cavagnolo, directly opposite the ship's prow. In the semidarkness, with a row of dilapidated houses looming behind it, half submerged in an automobile graveyard that stretched as far as the eye could see, it gave a menacing impression. I wouldn't have been surprised to hear a siren wail at any moment. In between the carcasses of vehicles, I saw human shadows loom up—bent figures, who must've been staying up late to dig for something among the metallic junk. And I knew too well what they were hunting for! Appropriately, I pretended not to see them.

The view was less distressing on the other side of the street: the houses were taller, the walls better preserved. I saw a factory for hair-dryer helmets, a shop selling plastic wares, a stationery shop and, what especially drew my attention, a little door standing open with the inside illuminated and a theater bill stuck to one of its panels—a very discreet notice. A sign was written above the door, in deliberately childish letters: PUPPET THEATER. The wall of the building that served as the theater had insulting graffiti smeared all over it in black paint. I went to the box office, and though the show had started long ago, I bought a ticket and headed inside. The little room was completely packed with regular people and lots of children. Theirs was a very different mood from what I'd seen on the street. They burst into laughter and applause, while on the tiny stage, two marionettes operated by wires—one representing a nineteenth-century general, the other a magisterial gentleman who could've been a minister in the Sardinian Parliament—were striking each other furiously with two huge clubs. It was the final scene, a duel to the death in the spirit of Carolingian-cycle heroics, its outcome still uncertain. Astonished, I saw that the "clubs" were two stiff wooden puppets. The general's name was Ettore de Sonnaz—the "Capataz"—while his opponent was Count Frederico Sclopis of Salerano—the "Mighty Saleran." They were clashing in the middle of a square, which I recognized as one of the squares in Turin. Each was struggling to get on the pedestal occupied by his opponent—that is, to switch places—but for all their efforts to beat each other into a pulp, neither of them was any closer to his goal. It was a very comical duel, worthy of the laughter I saw around me, and soon enough I joined in. Surrounding the duelists were other puppets, dressed as ordinary citizens, which they reached for, one at a time, to use as weapons. The spectators took sides in an impromptu chorus, with mock-heroic enthusiasm for this or that contender, and you could hear them shouting: "Sock 'im, Capataz!—Woo, that's the stuff, Saleran!" . . .

The title of the entertainment was: *The Twenty Days of Turin.*

I felt a sort of liberation realizing the methods this part of the neighborhood had found to express the "truth" of those lethal events. And they weren't just "alluding" to it, either. There was, you could say, a "visible respect" for the nitty-gritty.

> The COUNT and ETORRE drew arms, and they meant it!
> Not a soul in the Piazza was safe from their blitz.
> The two perpetrators came out undented,
> But the weapon of each bashed its partner to bits.

And then:

> Across the square the GENERAL now took flight;
> The COUNT behind him roared into the night!

This was a tense moment for the audience because it seemed the Count of Salerano was going to take the pedestal from the hated General and "at last have Via Juvarra to command." But the retreat was only a ruse, and "the stalemate rattled on, fresh pawns in hand." All very satisfying . . . Good show! It *would've* been, if only, right then, the floor hadn't started creaking: a gravelly, vindictive noise, which grew louder and louder. The puppeteer cut off in the middle of a verse as the stage lights blacked out. There came another sound, of breaking glass, and the theater was plunged into darkness . . . "Earthquake!" I heard someone shout as people pushed and shoved to escape the room. I was thrown to the floor, then straightened up and ran away too . . . Via Cavagnolo was filled with panic. Everyone was running down the street. There was a second tremor, more powerful but shorter-lasting, which seemed to affect mainly the car bodies piled up and the nearby houses . . . A very selective earthquake, it dawned on me . . .

In the side streets, in fact, the situation seemed different. One of these, Via Ivrea, gave no signs of agitation at all; all I saw were sportive young men wearing tights, standing in a neat line, each holding a walkie-talkie against his mouth and watching the scene of terror from below without any distress . . . The prow of the church remained in front of me, immense and shadowy . . . Then, little by little, everything calmed down. The tremors didn't repeat themselves; people started heading back into their homes, and at last even the sportive youngsters crept away from the scene. The show, however, didn't resume.

During the night I dreamed that a huge icebreaker had devastated the entire neighborhood.

The next morning, I arrived at Turin-Caselle Airport with a feeling of relief. I'd almost done it now. I just had to wait, in good trim, for the arrival of the shuttle bus that would carry me and the other passengers to the DC-10 standing on the runway. Men in orange jumpsuits were still fiddling around with the plane. Once I'd checked in my baggage and filled in my boarding card, two security officers determined that the case for my recorder (which I wanted to take on board with me) had no concealed weapons inside: the sight of my harmless instrument brought a smile to their faces. I still had a quarter of an hour before departure . . .

But what a horrible night it had been! It wasn't just my dream about Our Lady of the Straight-and-Narrow Path bulldozing houses and burying their tenants under rubble . . . (Its catastrophic work complete, the church shaped like the prow of a ship went back to its proper place, fully intact, only its prow was no longer a prow, but two giant hands folded blamelessly in prayer . . .) No, the nightmare wasn't the last of it . . . I was woken with a start, yet again, by another loud blow against the main door. This time, however, the entrance gave way. As I sat on the bed, my face pouring with sweat, I heard slow, lumbering foot-steps climb the staircase and halt in front of my bedroom door. I thought of dialing the emergency line so they'd dispatch a police car right away, but memories of my last encounter with Segre deterred me from trying it . . . What would I tell them over the phone? Could I even trust the cops? Maybe an ambulance would arrive the next day to take me to the loony bin . . . Then goodbye, Venice! Better to end my life like Giuffrida, strangled by two mer-ciless fingers . . . At worst, if that creature tried to break down my door and enter by force, I could dive out the window . . . Toward one o'clock, thankfully, it went away—*stomp! stomp!*—down the stairs, with more stomping out on the sidewalk and onto the road toward Gran Madre di Dio. As soon as the stomping faded away, I knew that I'd have nothing more to fear that night. That had to have been the last warning, all to make sure I had no second thoughts about leaving the city.

The shuttle bus came at last. As I climbed the ramp stairs into the plane, I noticed that a little crowd had turned up on the tarmac. How they'd gotten the extraordinary permission to do this, I didn't know. The people in the crowd waved with gusto at the passengers beside me, but nobody waved back. I looked at the gathering (. . . friends? . . . colleagues?) and saw that I was one of the passengers they were saluting. A blue foulard scarf was flapping in the wind just for me! And what a surprise when I realized the person waving it was Bergesio's sister! Two youngsters in navy blue suits, their faces already familiar, dealt me some kind of military salute with their wrists bent at right angles to their foreheads. And then, nestled a bit deeper among the others, I saw a figure in white with a sweet smile; she greeted me by fluttering her hand, almost like she was seeing off a lover . . . It was Sister Clotilde.

I didn't like this mise en scène one bit. I stepped inside the aircraft without responding to their compliments.

A female voice wished us a safe and happy journey on behalf of the captain and his crew; we were scheduled to land in Venice within roughly half an hour. Soon after that, the plane took off. I realized that there were no stewardesses moving through the aisles; nobody was going past to hand out the scented towelettes. The cockpit was closed off. The "safe and happy journey" announcement had been a recording. I'd never enjoyed air travel, and the neglect for the passengers shown by the aircrew had left me a little uneasy. Even so, the amount of anxiety my economy-class companions were displaying seemed excessive to me. They avoided speaking to each other or even looking at their fellow travelers. Instead, they clung to the armrests of their seats, keeping their mouths firmly shut or biting their lower lips. Not one of them had a newspaper open. If any of these people knew each other—by blood, by friendship, by marriage—then I should've seen at least a few of them holding hands: some glimpse of mutual consolation. But even a young couple, who could've been on their honeymoon, did nothing to ease one another's anxiety. Everybody kept to themselves, sitting alone in their fears. Yet the plane was flying quickly and evenly over a bank of clouds; the muffled whine of the engines was unbroken by turbulence; the regularity of the voyage couldn't have given rise to such dread. The aircraft tilted slightly on my side to correct its course, then returned immediately to its level position.

A shame the clouds prevented me from enjoying the scenery below. In the absence of any other diversions (I hadn't bought a newspaper) I gave myself over to drowsiness: well justified, considering how I'd spent the night. I fell into a deep sleep, free of dreams.

When I reopened my eyes, I saw that the plane was still in the air; it hadn't begun the landing preparations . . . I found this strange because I had a feeling I'd been sleeping for quite a while. I looked through the window and saw the sea below me, then another cloud bank, a rather large one, and then a flat, sandy landscape with no signs of habitation. The passengers didn't seem astonished by what was happening and carried on staring into space. Their eyes were a bit goggly, but I would say it was less a look of fear than of capitulation. I tried asking my neighbor for an explanation, but he shrugged without saying a word. Now the plane was descending. Certainly the overhead signs were lighting up: FASTEN YOUR SEAT BELT—NO SMOKING . . . But did anyone fasten

their belt? Was anyone smoking? Indeed, if I remembered properly, nobody had bothered with these precautions even during
takeoff; I was the only one who'd observed them . . . As the
plane's altitude dropped, the sandy expanse revealed itself to be a
desert of bumpy dunes. I thought we were making an emergency
landing and assumed the fetal position in my seat; but since the
other passengers kept leaning against their backrests, and since
I didn't want to be the only one crouching at that moment—or
make my fear obvious—I went back to peering out the window. I
could clearly see an airstrip now, and on it, the outline of another
plane. A group of people huddled together beside the aircraft, and
standing apart from them, in wondrous solitude, was an unmoving figure of exceptional height.

About twenty meters away from it there stood a second
statue, equally motionless.

The plane landed and came to rest at the far edge of the
runway—the extreme opposite of where the other DC-10 was
settled. The usual voice recording invited us to disembark.
When my feet touched the ground, I was stricken by a dreadful
heat wave: there wasn't a puff of cool air in this desert! Without
being ordered by anyone, my fellow travelers arranged themselves in pairs, and with an unsteady, shuffling gait, like a bunch
of slaves on a chain, they set off in the same direction . . . I lined
up with them too, no longer oppressed by the heat, but by a sense
of inevitability that prevented me from breaking away from the
"straight-and-narrow path" . . . I held my recorder in my hands
and remembered the smiles of the security officers at Caselle

Airport. There were no airports here! The only building was a wooden shack where some uniformed men sat under a canopy with their legs crossed, watching the scene impartially . . . Just as we arrived some few meters away from a being wearing a gray mantle, who stood with his back turned to us on a pedestal, the air became charged with a frightening tension . . . A dark force was draining me from within . . . The other giant figure stood twenty paces away; he went and plucked someone out from the group beside him, grabbed him by the hocks and, spinning the human like a club, he let out a terrible scream . . . His rival turned toward us. I saw his senile face, the face of a biblical prophet, his hair and long beard corroded by a pervasive blight. He stared through eyes devoid of pupils as if scanning the abysses of the past . . . Out of instinct, I put my recorder against my lips, and for what little I knew, I began to play it. From the depths of blackest despair, perhaps I'd manage to dig out a sound capable of soothing these powers. I was clutching at my last straw.

The Prophet was drawing near. Very shortly, the duel would commence . . .

—*October 1976*

APPENDIX I
THE DEATH AT MISSOLONGHI

A short story by Giorgio De Maria

Translated by Ramon Glazov

What follows is a private account by the Bishop Gualtiero Griffi of Venice, written in the December of 1879 and addressed to Cardinal Roberto Brancaleoni of Bologna, concerning an alleged episode in the life of Lord Byron:

I can see, Your Eminence, that your diocese is beset by many cares. How well I recognize the situation! I myself scarcely know where to turn anymore! But on this take my word: the backsliding of Venetian souls in my own bishopric has been truly dire! The Austrians in charge are doing everything within their purview, but for all their efforts, they are still far from omnipotent. We ought to have a duty constable and a priest standing watch over every home, but you, at least, should understand that this is beyond our earthly capabilities.

And the people, meanwhile, take advantage of this. Everywhere, their lechery finds niches which are rarely interfered with.

Wherever you look, there are patriots and radicals springing up like toadstools. That bane of the spirit known as "Romanticism" has infected a good part of our populace, bringing all its sad consequences. Their hearts are unruly, they have abandoned all human decency and—woe to report—they are very, *very* familiar with wickedness.

You have provided me, Your Eminence, with a truly valuable piece of news in describing how that shameful goat-footed poet came to dwell in your city and how the authorities brought this to your attention. Heaven would have wanted them to apprehend him and stop, at once and forever, the harm he has caused to unguarded minds! But I don't hold very high hopes of that happening. He is an Englishman, and the Austrians are unfailingly reluctant when it comes to laying a finger on one of those islanders. But what's more, our man is a lord, and for him this truly accidental fact serves as a form of insurance. As if highborn ancestors could keep a man from nursing the spirit of a crook and a tavern-lout! Your Eminence, have you read the things written about him in the London periodicals? He is said to be—and I quote—"a wretch whose organs, blunted by the habits and excesses of the most monstrous debauchery, can no longer find any means of excitement or stimulation except in the images of terror, suffering and destruction with which a crime-stained soul furnishes him only too easily"! Nothing, it seems to me, could lay him bare better than that. I thought much the same thing when I chanced to read some of his writings, which I tore to pieces at once before consigning them to the precious efforts of my fireplace . . . With that gesture, I felt almost as if I could stop his verses from selling like hotcakes and hamper the buyers from corrupting themselves in mind and body! (All the same, it would do well to acquaint certain constables in your native Bologna with that verdict from London: reading it will perhaps remove many of their qualms about the matter.)

☙❧

Still on the subject of that Englishman, have you heard what they've been saying about him in certain circles for quite some time now? I don't know how much of it is real or fabricated, but it seems positive to me that the story fits his character like a glove. You, having frequented the salons of Contessa Albizzi a few times in the past, would be the better one to judge if the gossip vented there is worth considering. I spoke about it to the Marquis of Zandonai during the last Feast of Precept when he came to visit me in the sacristy at the end of Mass. It truly is regrettable, Your Eminence, that your visits to Venice always have to be official ones and that you and I have never had the chance to wander around the city incognito for a while! I could introduce you to so many neighborhoods, to so many . . . people of interest. I'm not alluding to the Marquis of Zandonai, whom you already know, nor even to the palazzi which you used to frequent, but people rather much less visible, who could easily slip your notice if you're not "well up" on Venetian matters. You've already been here, I take it, and seen our "little streets"? And you also know the odor that permeates them, that singular smell! If corruption itself ever had a smell, that for sure would be it! Of course, the place is far from a pageant of sanitation, but how I wish we were dealing purely with *material* foulness!

The day before yesterday, I fancied taking the pleasure of delving into this urban maze where, here and there, I could gather the information which would allow me a clear vision of the strange story that has spread thinly round. It would indeed be worth your while if I digressed to tell you about several meetings I held, with people we've already spoken about at length, in our nostalgia for the informants of the Mouth of Truth—but that may have to wait for another time. I should also especially update you on certain scoundrels—known vulgarly as *"gnaghe,"* or "meowers"—who prowl around in cat masks disguised as women and spout obscenities which shock everyone around them. And what's particularly outrageous is they're tolerated: you don't see them merely in the piazza, but in the Procuratie, in the taverns and disorderly houses, at dances and celebrations, and it's said that their real craft is in sodomy. Foreigners attest that not even in Geneva, in a nation of Calvinists and Lutherans, is there anything like the scandal these *gnaghe* have caused, and that it would be best to arrest or forbid these masqueraders who practice rough trade, departing from the natural use of the woman which befits them. It was to one of those precise neighborhoods, where bordellos and gambling dens are plentiful, where I went two days ago to pause among people and listen to whatever came out of their mouths.

You must have heard of a certain Venetian neighborhood

called Frezzeria, which is quite well visited, not only as a place of unmentionable pastimes, but also as the spot where citizens gather to flog merchandise. It's lost some of its energy in recent decades as trade with the Orient has waned, but there are—as always—a few exotic objects to be found, which form the perfect lure for those tourists who yearn to primp their stately wives with some bauble from Syria or Lebanon, all so that their better halves can imagine they've really landed in one of those distant countries. It was there, in that same neighborhood, that the poet arrived three years ago—that poet who now flourishes in the shadow of your cathedral and stands poised to sow your diocese with the weeds that have already sprung up so rampantly here. For the first several months—before he and his seraglio of vultures and carrion crows withdrew under the roof of the Palazzo Mocenigo—the building where he lodged was a two-story dwelling, marred by centuries of wear and tear and by the neglect of its current proprietors. It's true that many things inside have been changed lately; you can see it especially in the upholstery and furnishings, both of which have gotten strangely refined, but, deferring such questions for now, the two proprietors are not personalities who seem much inclined toward cleanliness or decorum. The lady of the house herself is a woman of twenty-five, rather well heeled, who answers to the name of Marianna. She is rumored to have had many lovers, several of whom were even of the very basest extraction. Her husband, by contrast, is a man quite long in his years, tested harshly by life, with a past behind him filled with disappointments great and small which now envelop his existence like a swarm of reckless gnats. You would only need to look at his face to understand the burden on his memory to hold them all and to assign each one its proper weight and measure.

It would be worth your while, Your Eminence, to spare me a moment to describe this character, since everything that's recounted appears to have its origins with him.

✑✑

You need to know that before the arrival of the Englishman—the one who made the Saints turn pale with his catalogue of incests and adulteries perpetrated across Europe!—his future host kept a shop at the ground level of the house. I emphasize the word *before*, since today he doesn't seem to gain much through that enterprise: not, I'd judge, from the piles of clutter and dust which grow denser each day along the shelves of his shop. It's astounding even that he hasn't decided to close down the shop, but indeed to leave it open night and day, practically inviting any passing thieves to plunder it wholesale. Now you should be asking how this man could earn his livelihood, put food on the table for himself and his wife *and* find the ducats to beautify his house with hanging tapestries and that extortionate furniture. If the matter wasn't an enigma to me as well, then in all likelihood I wouldn't dwell in narrating these anecdotes which Prudence—first among the supreme cardinal virtues—would bid me to reject without delay as the fruit of lies and superstition.

But, at least for now, I'll keep to the details that are certain. I can say that the name of this man is Giuseppe and that he belongs to the Segati family, which was once renowned in our Most Serene Republic for its extensive trading with India and other territories in the Orient. However, the dynasty later fell into decline, to the point of having no assets save for that very homely curiosity shop where our Giuseppe—the last scion of his house—carried out an activity which, in truth, wasn't very lucrative until a few months ago. Just one sign of the small esteem this man held compared to his spouse was the nickname she seemingly gave him in the first few days of their marriage. Women have a most subtle talent for pondering names that could mortally wound the men they hold in contempt, and she could not have thought of anything more merciless to inflict him with than a second Baptism, a second naming more inerasable than the first. It's said she nicknamed him the "Straggler-Cat" for the way he used to maunder from room to room without a sound, as cats, in their muffled manner, have a habit of doing. You'll know the grievous insult in this if you consider that Giuseppe, with his hefty figure and sagging features, has scarcely anything feline about him; at most, you can summon to mind the image of a very ancient cat who's had too much of catching mice and, instead of nestling down in some distant corner as would be natural in such cases, drags his tired limbs around the house in an altogether vain attempt to hide his decrepitude. It's enough, though, just for that man to come to the dinner table for all of his physical frailty to display itself: there's no broth, no salad dish he'll ingest without a grimace of pain etched on his lips. Nor does he have much appetite for table talk, except to ask about minor developments—who'll sing in the role of Orfeo at the Teatro La Fenice, how this or that distant relative is faring— and often as not his young wife will abandon him to solitude, perhaps after serving him with a dry or hurtful answer.

ജ്യ

One day—after having asked her husband again and again why he was in the habit of leaving the house on certain nights of the year, and just as the Christmas holidays were drawing near—she didn't hesitate to fall silent herself and follow after him as soon as she noticed him stepping past the threshold of his quarters. And when she saw him descend to the street level where the shop lies—then step outside, donning one of the masks citizens wear during Carnevale—she found herself so curious that she decided to shadow him in the laneways through which he advanced. Now, having observed him heading toward Giudecca, and entering a small chapel which was known to host assemblies of the most impudent characters in Venice, she robed herself the following evening in garments more appropriate for eavesdropping at close quarters. Over her face she placed a gentleman's *baùtta* mask and adopted the kind of disinterested strut that allows the occasional outsider to penetrate certain secret gatherings, including this very particular meeting where, amid the smell of incense and candles, prayers were raised to a divine Cupid surrounded by shepherds, and where the sound of panpipes sometimes drifted beside whispered devotions. And we can picture her surprise, as well, when she spied her husband getting up from his pew and kneeling before a pagan altar, where he raised his arms skyward—if one could call the blue fresco of that ceiling a sky—and, in the silence which had quickly overtaken the chapel, reciting melancholy verses.

There is no poorer man in the world than one who faces the sudden airing of that secret which, for him, is the only receptacle where he can keep the flame of his vanity lit—so that he doesn't start to resemble a pitiable shrub, winter-stricken by frost and blizzards. And there's no woman of bad intent who doesn't know how to make use of a cold blade which, by fate or by craft, she now has in her hand. Just as she was able to find the destination of his nocturnal walks, she also sniffed out where he hid the fruits of his Arcadian laments. There wasn't a drawer in the house or in the shop she didn't frantically rummage through, keen to unearth what her husband had hoped to hide from her feminine malice. And when, at last, a bundle of well-preserved parchment scrolls fell into her hands, few people in the district were unaware of what this occult activity said about a man whose domestic fate was well-known gossip; many began to treat him to a snicker as they passed by his shop, whose sign—in a hostile collusion of apathy and destiny—was a *horn*, to be exact, a large hunting horn painted in gold. He caught on to their mockery from behind his counter shrouded in twilight, and we too can visualize how green his face became at hearing his pagan elegies callously repeated by figures in the street. Nor was there a lack of pranksters who pinned to his door certain writings from Lombardy at the time, reproving those followers of Classicism who never tire of scratching around in the ashes of the Ancient World, who still fancy that the lost paintings of Parrhasius bear the truest promise of earthly beatitude . . . And their foolish illusion is properly savaged in those biting verses by the Lombard laureate Carlo Porta, whose Milanese pagan (or "Meneghin Classegh") declares:

> Minerva consoles me through my daily chores,
> Morpheus tucks me in and bids me sleep,
> Bacchus warms my heart and helps me to forget.

This was the situation our "Straggler-Cat" found himself in when my native city saw the arrival of that poet whom Nature, from the moment of his birth, seemed to have stamped with a mark of baleful predestination. He arrived in a carriage drawn by four majestic horses, so that, seeing him halt at the limits of the city, people gazed at him with the same wonder which must have stricken the crowds of olden times when the Bucentaur set sail from the Basin of San Marco. But this was the amazement of servile minds ensnared by the false luster of celebrity, not of devout and humble souls. He only had to step down from the carriage for men of all ages to swarm around him, prostrating themselves to the point of licking the ground and seizing his hand to kiss it, almost as if it carried the Piscatory Ring of His Holiness, and immediately they offered him all kinds of services. Yet he, with the air of an individual who sought nothing but to reaffirm his strength and prestige, quickly shooed off that parasitic crowd, and, leaving the horses and carriage in a stable, he made for the canals with only his luggage. Having disembarked at St. Mark's Square, it took him little time to come across an opportune hostel, so foolproof is a libertine's instinct for finding promising terrain. So he reached Frezzeria and, admiring the freedom with which many well-bred ladies went strolling in the evening, accompanied by their stylish servants, and finding himself enticed by the aroma that blew from certain coffee shops, where it was difficult to distinguish a high-born dame from a woman of the world, he immediately decided that this, for now, was the right place to put down his unsavory roots. He requested and obtained lodging in the house of the merchant, and under its roof he stayed, long enough to violate every rule of decency and common living.

☙❧

Thus far, Your Eminence, I would not appear to have said anything in the least bit contentious or liable to doubt. Nor will I depart from the stringent truth by describing the room where the poet lived and wrote some of his most famous and celebrated verses, as a tiny, unadorned room with nothing except for a bed, a couple of chairs and a desk. It indeed seems that, time and again, those souls plagued by Romanticism find a supreme thrill in the simulation of poverty, in donning the robes of the friar, all to allow the flames of their lust to excite them better and more underhandedly. I shall not ponder for long, either, whether that dwelling had a Bible and a missal-book along with the furniture I've listed, or if one could find even one sonnet dedicated to the Blessed Virgin Mary within that poet's vast works.

His enemies say that he loves only what he has to escape from, that genuine emotions are not enough for him and that he is never so pleased as when he sees the shadow of death overhanging the nuptial bed where he lies. Similar shadows must have festooned our city, whose obvious decline might perhaps have disappointed those with simple tastes, but not our Englishman: "I have been familiar with ruins too long to dislike desolation." And ruins and desolation were what he found, and where he didn't find them, he took every means to create them.

℘

He wrote back to one of his cronies in England that, in his eyes, Venice was a "bewitching city," and "the greenest island of my imagination." So freely could the whims of a Romantic lend alluring color to the miasmal bogs that were ready to swallow him whole! In his usual error—or gazing with an eye that ignored the counsel of his mind—he even humored himself to describe the woman with whom he would unite in sin, as "altogether like an antelope; she has the large black oriental eyes, with that peculiar expression in them which is seen rarely among Europeans— even the Italians—and which many of the Turkish women give themselves by tinging the eyelids, an art not known out of that country, I believe." And again he indulged in over-portraying her, "mouth small—skin clear and soft, with a kind of hectic colour," failing indeed to observe that the hint of purple enlivening her cheeks was a thing she owed not to hectic fever—in barer words, *consumption*—but to the open air and hot sun she caught from afternoon strolls along the marina, none of which were any cure for the impropriety of her nature. But whatever judgments he made regarding the aforesaid woman, he rarely strayed from the truth writing about the love he felt for her, especially since she agreed to share his bed at any time of his choosing, a convenience which a man of his temperament was highly inclined to welcome.

I won't linger, Your Eminence, in describing their communion; if sublime words ever came from anywhere, it was not from the closed circle of carnal embrace. Nor will I dwell on relating how their idle hours were spent by day, nor the nights consumed in the vain but deadly fires of their misdeed, nor the spite, resentment and the jealousy that haunted their lovemaking as an omen of a more eternal tempest. On several occasions she was seen outside, flustered and upset as if her soul was at the point of breaking, or tearing at the shoulder of her footman and, with no warning, showering him in the most vicious abuses that have ever risen from a woman's lips. But the blistering grievances she spat seemed like trifles to the poet. He only had to gaze at her sweetly to draw her to him again like a mellow yeanling, and, with a short-lived caress, to put her back in her accustomed yoke.

ᗱᗩ

The unhappy merchant endured his wife's betrayal as only an ambitious, disappointed, love-struck and helpless man could endure such a thing. A cute tale, spun by the evil-minded, claims that the Straggler-Cat was a creature incapable of true suffering, and that his tears were no more valid in the court of human woes than the weeping of sopranos in stage melodramas. That mean prejudice would have been shattered had anyone drawn close enough to view the terrible bite marks which can still be seen gouged into the wood of his kneeler, or certain scratches which remain on the furniture in his shop for any sharp-eyed visitor to notice—not to speak of recollections which people still trade about the solitary walks he took on sunny afternoons, dragging his feet and brushing close to the wall. His partial self-exile from the sight of his domestic spouse must have happened very early, and perhaps it came more out of instinct or lazy discretion than at his wife's explicit urgings. Yet all the same, there had to be crucial moments in the day when the three of them could not avoid coexisting. And these are precisely the moments which the town gossip—cultivated and vulgar alike—has been most drawn to in its anecdotes and speculations:

The Marquis of Zandonai told me, for instance, that the friends of Contessa Albizzi liked to imagine the trio supping in the most nervous of silences, with the Straggler-Cat bent over his plate and unwilling to raise his eyes for fear of meeting the uncouth gaze of the poet—that face crossed with free-hanging hairs in which Marianna loved to glimpse the fascinating hiero-glyphs of Heroic Destiny. Those inclined to cruder fantasies may prefer to think of a scene torn by a much harder contrast of power: the legitimate husband in a corner, taking his soup, while the other two, drinking together from the same cup, laugh and point at him. But in every case, the inequality of the two contend-ers always springs to our attention. Nor would we drift too far from reality if we imagined how they spent one of their evenings together. The poet has just finished reciting one of his incandes-cent verses, and his mistress, still swept with emotion, turns to her husband and asks: ". . . and now, Straggler-Cat, dear, why don't *you* try reciting some of your lovely verses?" Whatever hap-pened, the limits of human tolerance must have been breached a good many times if what they say isn't a complete myth.

ɢⱴꙊ

Conceivably, you have read or heard a certain poem, Your Emi-nence, which the Englishman happened to complete in my city. The poem describes a magician locked within the walls of an alpine castle inhabited by spirits and demonic beings, whose shad-owy, arcane presences came to him obediently in the vast silence of those icy mountains. More, you would recall what happened when the magician, laid low by awful remorse over his incestu-ous crimes, asked not for more power, but to forget who he was and enjoy the deepest oblivion—and how none of these things were granted. Neither the melodious apparition of the Witch of the Alps, nor of the kinswoman he had taken in illicit love, was sufficient comfort for his soul tormented by regrets. An abbot tried to give him solace with modest and holy words, but not even these could make his proud spirit ask for the forgiveness which would have been the only release from his afflictions. As arrogant to God as he was to the Evil One, he preferred to die rejecting everyone and everything rather than bow his forehead. Nor do we know if death gave him the oblivion he sought. And as pitiless as that creature was, so too was the man who aspired to be the thing his imaginings had produced.

They say that he was still laboring over that very poem when his pen suddenly stopped as if stricken by a pitiless enchantment. Now a very different oblivion from what his hero Manfred had sought for fell over his mind and held him from bringing the dramatic work to a close. It often happens that poets spoiled by Romanticism project themselves into the personalities they happen to create, and after having aggrandized these mannequins, they fancy themselves aggrandized in turn. Or perhaps, after conjuring the Devil with their quills and envisaging his presence, black wings and all, they fancy themselves worthy to have him appear before them just as they'd pictured. This is ignoring of course that the Father of Lies knows far subtler arts of manifestation, and revealing himself so baldly gives him no pleasure.

ↄ⌇ↄ

So our poet had spent his days versifying and chasing skirts, until that strange, and perhaps even faintly miraculous, event.

ൈ

Of those who saw the merchant during that ordeal, a few mentioned him to me with that ironic indifference people adopt, out of habit, to describe men stricken by conjugal misfortune. They were, indeed, rather sparing in their accounts of his tribulations and their cause. Some even seemed to hold back from fear of revealing details which—though they weren't quite sure—nonetheless caused them to suspect something horrifying and arcane. And I could tell you that I was just conferring with a face from that locality when a window sprang open above our heads and the very subject of our discussion appeared. And since he was watching us both so intently, my friend shut his mouth and left me, running as fast as he could. What could suddenly have entered those eyes which, years before, had only been cause for laughter and pity, eyes so soft and helpless that they seemed to shrink into their sockets if others met their stare? Suffering allows no rest for the man who becomes its prey; but, as often happens to the animal that hears the barking of hounds behind it and yet manages to evade capture—its terror-sharpened eye finding a path through the foliage which brings it momentary salvation—so a man can sometimes happen to find solace in an action or gesture that soothes his anguish but briefly.

It was a bright afternoon in summer when the merchant, by now well hounded by his torments, suddenly found himself of a mind to break his humiliating routine—so much so, indeed, that I might be permitted to think that what followed wasn't entirely his own doing. Neither Ruzzante the Paduan nor the Roman Plautus had ever described marital distresses as sordid and laughable as those he'd lived through. And since it pleased the Englishman to no end to intensify the scorn of others as a condition to his own delight, one often heard his thundersome voice heaving abuses at the miserable shadow that loitered around, uncertain if it could still recognize the house as its own. But what could our Amphitryon do when the Jupiter in his home had barred the door to him, all the better to enjoy his wife? And perhaps some demonic intercession had even allowed this! Now was the scheduled hour when the private congress between the poet and Marianna reached its height of passion, and no person—especially not the merchant—would have dared disturb its murky sanctity. The house, as ever, was silent and an immodest twilight reigned over it. What gave our Straggler-Cat the boldness to choose that precise time to intrude into his own dwelling and swiftly climb the stairs is beyond the guess of any man who has never held such intimate shame in his heart. But he dared to do it, and, pressed by a blinding fury, he came close to that door which, as if on the sly, his imagination had breached many times. None could say now if he gripped a weapon in his hand or if his fainthearted valor was the sole armament, but once the door was open, nothing save for his eyes would shred the nestling couple. Venus—as it's said in Lucretius—had already *sown the fields of woman* and already the lovers were pressed anxiously tight, tooth to amorous tooth, when the poet raised his head and saw the Straggler-Cat watching him. He said nothing, but his exhausted carnality yielded to the concentrated power of hatred and pain that shot from those once meek and fearful eyes. He tried then to cover his limbs, but the more of his miserable nudity the blanket hid, the more he felt he was exposing: that stare, which had become diamond-sharp, cut deep into his suddenly transparent being and opened vast and hidden wounds within it. And, as it happens in a city whose battlements are crumbling under a determined onslaught, when its citizens cling to each other while enemies rush in to carry out their plunder and devastation, so the poet clung to his woman. But that wretched filial gesture proved almost worthless to impede the silent claws that would dig into his depths, which were now open as daylight, and steal their unguarded treasures. He lay on that bed exactly like a thirsty man in a dream who has consumed every trace of water and now sits dying of thirst in the middle of a river. Nor do we know how long he remained there: only after the merchant had left with his hands full from an intangible robbery did he come around and find himself stripped of everything, in a confined solitude, forgetful and speechless.

Your Eminence, our late lamented Bishop Alfonsini, while speaking one day to a crowd of poets, musicians and painters who had agreed to hear him at St. Mark's Basilica, said well that what we call "personality" is nothing more than a theft, and that it is the sum of foolishness to take pride in this supposed quality.

Those who expect to turn their personality into an excuse for rebellion against human and divine laws are, in reality, behaving like gypsies who, having taken away some elegant garment or some precious necklace from others, now adorn themselves with it, and, finding their presence in the mirror more beautiful or captivating than it was before, do not hesitate to imagine that they have suddenly transformed into queens or gentlefolk. Indeed these goods only have to be repossessed for them to newly find themselves in all the misery and nakedness of their natural state. For verily only those who renounce themselves, and refuse to look at the bounties of Creation with eyes clouded by avidity and false desire, shall enter the Kingdom of Heaven, where all things are clear and pure.

ॐ

The life the three of them shared wasn't broken up as suddenly as one might expect after what had occurred; they still had their suppers together—many, many suppers—and their solitary walks and secret dialogues continued all the same. If something had changed, it was in the balance of their coexistence, as if some force had intervened to shift the weights on an invisible scale. The poet's nights of musing and creative toil—the fruits of which Marianna was always the first to taste—changed so severely that they lost all their hallowed quietude, exchanging it for the sound of pacing feet, torn paper and barren sighs. Even his morning rides along the coast, where the artist mingled his self-love with the contemplation of the waves, lacked the blusterous security they once held and turned swift and convulsive. His outbursts of rage and joy alike were smothered under a gray fog.

✍

Once, while he was trying in vain to continue the work he had set into motion, his mistress approached him unseen and, folding her arms around his neck, she uttered his name in a smitten, coquettish tone. If the poet's fit of anger still betrayed a virile urge to rebel, even this barrier fell when his head sank into the woman's lap and stayed there. And his hands just as often seemed given to hers while they sat wordless in a box seat at the theater. Against the merchant, they were more than just a pair of lovers facing a betrayed spouse; they now behaved like two creatures seeking a defensive stronghold in the shape of a common alliance. The man's presence had lost its old circumspection, and even if his footsteps remained hushed, he no longer hesitated to appear in front of them and give sidelong glances. He circulated through the household looking like a black beetle that comes into view from a place no one is sure of and disappears somewhere just as uncharted. One day, the poet stood alone on a balcony, gazing out at Venice's generous expanse, where he hoped to recover the lost voice of his poetry. All of a sudden he winced as a foretoken of the images he yearned for seemed to be reborn in his mind. A smile had already come back to his lips and he was already preparing to put the suggestions of his insight to paper, when a dark

167

power emerged to rob him of his premonitions with a greedy suction. The Englishman spun around just in time to see the merchant retreat behind an awning with the ravenous motion of a beast clutching warm prey between its teeth. And because at other times he sensed a predator at his back, he came to fear his landlord's absence as much as his presence. It was often the case that he and Marianna would call out for him if they didn't see his figure hunkering nearby. The merchant himself would respond quickly to their calls and straightaway reveal himself with a modest, "What is it?" But at night—while the Straggler-Cat did his mysterious and solitary work inside the shop—Marianna lay in her bed and listened to the poet's agitated pacing echo through the house, and, never daring to move and join him, she let the sound of footsteps nourish her pained slumber.

☙

What happened next, when the frail membrane of suspense which had enclosed their coexistence like a shell finally burst, stirs me almost with horror to recount. It was another evening with the trio sitting at the customary table. Not one of them had as yet said a word. Only the candlesticks gave life to their three presences by the fidgeting of magnified shadows on the walls, and only the faraway *slap-slap* of lagoon waters breached the silence. Everything seemed to be unfolding just like the evening before, when the Straggler-Cat launched into a coughing fit that suggested he was about to make some trifling household discussion. Then, in an accent one would use for everyday table talk, he began to recite certain verses in Venetian. Marianna, who didn't recognize these rhymes as her husband's usual mediocrity, stood stiff like a gazelle that had heard roaring nearby. The poet too repeated the words to himself and turned pale. Watching them and pretending not to notice their shock, building more and more dramatic emphasis and almost relishing his intonation, the merchant continued the strophe he had started. Perhaps it was a gesture incited by fear, or perhaps the poet was ashamed, from hearing in such a slovenly recital the words he had long and fruitlessly pursued for his *Manfred*, enough that it roused him to grasp the end of his tablecloth and take cover behind it as if finding himself suddenly naked. Other words, other verses, piled on without pause, in somewhat garbled diction.

There is no telling, Your Eminence, if seeing an idea of one's own—a personal notion one has not yet brought to full maturity—suddenly unveiled in a distorting mirror is an experience any man could endure. Few indeed have ever tried. But from what they say, it does not seem the Englishman took it well. The scene that followed, in fact, was a frenzy of paroxysmal movements. Some recount it as a wheezing chase around the table, where the merchant slurred verse after verse while the poet begged him in vain to put an end to the costly spillage; others say instead that the poet threw himself at the merchant in an instant and took him by the throat, hoping that this would arrest the grandiose flow of those words which had grown into a mighty cascade. I could scarce know which of the many versions told might be closest to infallible truth. But it seems the more probable to me that the merchant was able to escape his opponent's grip and dwindle away from the room. Now the poet and his woman were very desperate to track him down. There are some who claim to have spotted the pair as they combed the streets that night, asking left and right if by chance anyone had seen him. And people even now recall their shallow breath, their fluttering hither and thither like moths around an oil lamp. When at last they found him, he was locked in a wine cellar inside the house and our poet had no choice left but to stop feebly and listen. From inside, the merchant's voice poured out in abundance, oratorical one moment, hasty and monotonous the next. The Englishman tried beyond hope to take what he heard to memory and save some word or two. Rivers of poetry . . . unborn . . . *prenascent* . . . pelted through that door, perhaps vanishing without a second chance to be heard; nor was there a human shorthand swift enough to jot them down. All that night the poet stood there, to listen and to hear *himself,* with his hands outspread like a beggar. Only when dawn came again was he able to move and climb slowly back up the stairs, almost like a shade, sapped of all he had been.

☙❧

At this you should ask, Your Eminence, how that husk of a man still happens to enthrall the masses, to sell poems and to be a prolific and celebrated wordsmith. If his whole store of rhymes and images had perished that night, then perhaps I wouldn't worry myself too deeply over his destiny and the ruination his presence in the world even now serves to propagate. I would leave him to his fate, to chase whatever shallow death awaits him in some far-off land. But such is certain, however, that he has not remained entirely quiet, and that the lengthiest poems still jet out from his pen. You must be conscious of his *Don Juan* and of his *Manfred*, both taken skillfully to completion, and other works of his lately published to sizable admiration. It happens at times that men can outlive themselves and persevere, like wraiths, by carrying out the actions they have always carried out; their souls are mute but not their voices, and their hands and feet do not stop moving. Seeing them in the street or riding in the saddles of their chargers, no one would think that their minds had lost their hum, that the blood in their veins was heatless and spent; nor do the women they still hold tight to their bosoms ever imagine such a tremendous absence . . . And in the city there's no lack of them . . . Often, even, the more the vacuum inside them is pierced, the more grandiosely they act, giving shows of themselves, fashioning great spectacles of gaiety, dauntlessness and brio. There's never a Carnevale in Venice where their masks don't make an appearance. And if times and manners continue to slide as they do now, it shall not be long before these walking husks will form great crowds, whose presence no one will be able to evade.

In the meantime, I can tell you that so far our Englishman hasn't stopped making hasty and sporadic jaunts here in Venice. No one—at least, not anyone who isn't in the know about his intimate secrets—would recognize him during *these* visits. Because

Venice for him is a realm of humiliation, he hesitates to come here with his features so changed, like a leper who doesn't wish to be pointed out. What could he still hope to do or find in this place, that he hasn't done or gotten already? It's painful to answer that kind of question. He does, at any rate, bring himself here, and after nightfall, he approaches the merchant's house and knocks a number of times as a recognized signal. The door can be seen opening and the merchant leans out just a little; with a quick wave of his hand he bids his guest into the quiet of the house, where they both remain for a few short moments. So indeed it stipulates, the unsavory pact which binds them, and has bound them since that night. The Englishman divests himself of a bag of money; the merchant, a bag of parchment scrolls. What they discuss among themselves cannot be anything two mortals should ever say to each other *in this life*. Their sad haggling complete, the Englishman pulls away from the house and dissolves into the murk without breathing a word. Certainly, whatever *is* written on the scrolls could sound nothing like his mother tongue; but it serves him little to shed tears over so much infidelity if they nonetheless contain the works that ought to have been his. Arriving as he will at some outlying hostel, far from the inquisitive glances of his friends and the crowd, he will begin to unravel that priceless bundle at once. And then his pen shall stand ready to translate his verses from that humble dialect into his native English. Once that barren struggle comes to a close, others will undertake to publicize it and to entrust it to the wings of fame. Can it incite much wonder, then, that the Englishman's assets continue to dwindle and his castle at Newstead is no longer the crown jewel of his estate? Or that the Venetian merchant has so quickly shaken the grip of his old privations?

I can leave you no more, Your Eminence, save my word that these things are told in Venice, and that, in all humility, I have tried for nothing save a dependable summary,

Ever Yours, Most Faithfully,

BISHOP GUALTIERO GRIFFI

Appendix II
Phenomenology of
the Screamer

An essay by Giorgio De Maria

Translated by Ramon Glazov

[*Translator's Note: The term "screamer" in this piece is a literal rendering of the Italian* urlatore—*pl.* urlatori—*a wave of energetic pop-rock singers who emerged in Northern Italy at the start of the 1960s and have rough cousins in French yé-yé, the early Beatles and certain Jacques Brel tunes such as "Mathilde."*

Though 1960s jukebox hits seem mild compared to the rock genres that would succeed them, De Maria's extraordinarily visceral analysis of the "screamer" phenomenon gives an early taste of the subjects that would obsess him in the darker period when he conceived The Twenty Days of Turin.]

In an interview with the singer Tony Dallara reproduced below,[*] we find certain statements that might provide an inroad to understanding the near-magical allure of the "screamer" ballad—

_____

[*] From a conversation between the author and Tony Dallara, recorded at the Circolo Aurora in Collegno on the seventh of December 1960:

an allure that has proven especially strong for the younger generations.

Dallara, in short, doesn't believe there's anything new or surprising about the genre he is said to have "invented." Youngsters like him were fed up with soppy tunes where they kept stumbling across the word "love" and the tears of rejected crooners. They demanded something else, something that agreed better with their youthful impulses. Dallara being, by his own definition, a

---

GIORGIO DE MARIA: Do the lyrics of a song feel important to you?

TONY DALLARA: Very important. The music and lyrics have to blend well for a good song to succeed.

GDM: In other words, the lyrics mean something too?

TD: Today, yes. The public pays attention to the words. But once upon a time, no, because the songs back then were all identical, all copies of each other like they came from the same mold. All the songs spoke about love, about kisses, "my treasure"; and the melodies were all identical, tedious, always the same thing; even the crooners had to sing, all of them, in the same style. But today, no—finally! Because these are songs that come straight from the hearts of young people like us. We've adapted them and sung them how we wanted. And now, as things are today, we listen to music and words alike, and they are very important.

[. . .]

GDM: What advice would you give to a singer who's just starting out?

TD: For a singer who's just starting out, my first word of advice would be not to imitate anyone—if they want to have a personality, if they want to become somebody. They have to first of all sing what they feel; they shouldn't let themselves be influenced, but instead they should sing differently from other people. If they don't do that, they'll never be anything.

GDM: Do they have to believe in what they're singing? If they deliver a song that's powerfully sad or dramatic, do they have to be sad themselves or does it make no difference if they don't give a hoot?

TD: That's a different case from singer to singer. There's the singer who wants to make a craft out of singing, and he does it; from the moment he cries or laughs, he does what he has to do. But I, following my own approach, always sing about myself. However I sing, that's what my feelings are; in other words, I'm not capable of invention. If I have to say something, I sing it. I'm completely sure of what I sing, and if I wasn't, I wouldn't sing it.

"truthful" singer, incapable of affectation, did nothing more than listen to his instincts and take charge. The result was that his songs, almost by magic, seemed revolutionary: capable, that is, of quenching his unruly desires and those of his audience.

The conviction with which our singer-songwriter spoke about "sincerity," with regards to his own way of doing things and to screamers in general, implied that this much-vaunted sincerity perhaps held the secret of the matter. And that his "taking charge" was little more than a better way to reveal and expose whatever still lay unexposed and unrevealed. Compared to his fellow screamers, then, the old crooners would seem like individuals trapped in a kind of melodious prudery. They were close to being hypocrites, never daring to express in plain words all the things that their songs implied.

From analyzing literary texts, we have seen how forcefully the element of narcissism appears in Italian popular music, blossoming from a state of near-endless frustration. So, to examine the screamers as the spiritual renovators of the Italian pop song, we need to consider the "scream factor" itself, endowed with powers that are unique in their own right, which the devotees of crooning had perhaps lacked. But it's precisely this "scream factor" that leads us to suppose that if something new has happened in the music world, it's not a case of evolution, but a regression to a psychological state that had already existed.

A scream, on its own—when it doesn't indicate a genuine discovery of the world, full of childlike wonder—seldom means anything joyful. The voices within the song, high-pitched and strident, are often a musical emblem of pain. The musicologist Alan Lomax noted this studying the voices of Mediterranean folk-singers from Spain and Southern Italy*—regions saddled with strong sexual repression. While the songs of northern peoples (referring, of course, to traditional works and not commercial pop) lean toward deep voices and relaxed melodies, in southern cultures the anguish of repression manifests itself in songs that are strident with frequent wailing. If the cause for our own screamers' anguish is found in the lifestyle imposed by Northern Italy's industrialized society, rather than in the moral traditions of the peasant south, we still can't deny that a similar agitation exists deep within them. And perhaps the following passage from Lomax could be said just as well for the disciples of Adriano Celentano and Tony Dallara:

> The day we fully learn the relationship between the vocal means essential to the expression of the emotions and how these connect to styles of singing, another big step will have been made in the field of scientific musicology. But in this particular case—regarding vocalists in Southern Italy—a few preliminary observations can be shared with the reader. When a human being lapses into an outburst of intense pain, it emits a series of sustained, doleful notes in an extremely shrill voice.

---

* Alan Lomax, "Nuova ipotesi sul canto folkloristico nel quadro della musica popolare mondiale," in *Nuovi Argomenti*, pp. 17–18, Rome, November 1955–February 1956.

PHENOMENOLOGY OF THE SCREAMER

Grown adults too, just like children, scream in pain. To do this, the head is cast back and the jaw thrust forward; the soft palate draws near to the throat; the uvula tightens so that a small stream of air bursts out at high pressure to the top, vibrating the hard palate and the sinus. An easy try-at-home experiment ought to convince anyone that this is the best way to scream or moan. If, in the midst of it, you should open your eyes slightly (because if you've tried following my instructions they will be closed automatically) you will see your brow furrowed, your face and neck reddened, the facial muscles under your eyes pinched tight and your throat stretched by the effort.

༄༅

The lyrics of screamer songs, those composed at least when the trend had already made its mark on sales, reveal their emotional origin clearly enough. Such goes for the song "Hate" ["L'odio"], which could well be considered the "Manifesto of Screamerism":

> Hate is all that burns in my heart,
> After the love comes the hate!
> [. . .]
> (FROM "L'ODIO" BY U. BINDI/G. CALABRESE)

And much of that negative tension remains unaltered, even when the language being hurled about is otherwise tender.

Such is the case with the Domenico Modugno song "Millions of Sparks" ["Milioni di scintille"], where the lover, having erupted into a flurry of schizoid imagery all because his favorite girl told him yes, overwhelms his song with repetitions of, "She said yes! She said yes! She said yes!" which are gradually lost in a limbo of onanistic desperation.

While in old crooner songs the "smoldering desire" was often veiled in allegory and softened by the melody, the new screamer compositions announce it in more explicit terms. *"I want you, I want you, I want only you,"* the rumba-rocker sings. *"It's you I want,"* and he adds: *"The joy, the agony, the fever—my desire for you is burning—because I want you—I want you to be mine."* The singer never happens to reach the object of his yearnings, but the song finally quietens into satiety. The bowstring of desire tenses back almost to the brink of snapping, and that's where it stays, showing the lover caught in the throes of his spasm, yet perversely happy to display his state to others.

The typical fan of this genre isn't content to hear it at a normal sound level. Rather, he feels a need to raise the speaker volume to its maximum limits, as if hoping to remove every obstacle between himself and the screamer. His is not the attitude of a person who listens to music and contemplates it, but of someone who immerses himself physically in its element and yearns to form a part of it. The screamer, with his anonymous spasms, is the listener himself with his indiscriminate sexuality; the effrontery of the voices erupting from the jukebox is the same effrontery as the listener's, who, by virtue of the example he has been given, can finally shed the veils of his modesty. It might be said that screamer songs allow their audiences to strip bare while remaining clothed, to taste all the sordid thrills of carnal exhibitionism without officially crossing the line. It is, indeed, a kind of sanctioned transgression. The fact then that we are dealing not with an open, freely vented sexuality, but a repressed, wishful desire, reveals precisely the vocal style used by the screamers: intense, almost strangled at birth, as if a contradictory force were preventing it from expanding according to its natural cadence. It is here that we find a "sincere" rejection of the non-spontaneous.

And yet the songs *scream*, which—more than in any other popular music today—prompts the thought of an inward petrification, a coagulating interior, sometimes following the path of a rhythmic scheme that might even carry more than just a vocal or muscular spasm. Examining the lyrics of some of the latest songs in the genre, we could say that there is at least the attempt to exorcise the petrification, to escape it somehow. And here lies an ominously amusing side to the screamers.

Let's take the example of a successful "cha-cha-cha" song, "When the Moon is Full" ("Quando c'è la luna piena," A. De Lorenzo/G. Malgoni). We can observe three new features that contrast with tunes from the so-called "melodistic" or crooner repertoire: (1) the abolition of the chorus, (2) the lack of rests or pauses in the melodic pattern, (3) the stream of notes almost hitting back at each other, or at least with minimal space between them.

What should we read from innovations like these? What are the screamers aspiring for in their displays of rhythm? The recurrence of rhythmic sounds, duplicated obsessively and at length, have a noted effect on human beings. In his book *The Story of Jazz*, critic Marshall Stearns describes how during a visit to Haiti he had the good fortune of attending a primeval ceremony where:

> For three or more hours, the *housnis*, or priestesses, danced and sang a regular response to the *houngan's* cries, while the drum trio pounded away hypnotically. In a back room was an oven-like altar. Within the oven was a tank of water containing a snake, sacred to Damballa, and on top of this altar was a second, smaller one, containing a blonde baby doll of the Coney Island variety and a statuette of the Madonna, twin symbols of Ezulie, goddess of fertility and chastity.
>
> About eleven o'clock the lid blew off. Drinking from a paper-wrapped bottle, the *houngan* sprayed some liquid out of his mouth in a fine mist and the *mambos*, or women dancers, became seized with religious hysteria, or "possessed," much like an epileptic fit. The rest of the group kept the "possessed" ones from hurting themselves. I saw one young and stately priestess, who had earlier impressed me with the poise and dignity of her dancing, bumping across the dirt floor in time with the drums. The spirit of Damballa, the snake god, had entered her.*

Most likely, the screamers also hope to attain this kind of

---

* Marshall Stearns, *The Story of Jazz*, Oxford University Press, New York, 1956.

"possession," an epileptic seizure that would at last free them from their possibly unbearable emotive tension. Except that *their* final payoff is nipped in the bud. The screamer indeed follows—if only to a modest extent—a pattern common to certain primordial ceremonies (of which Marshall Stearns's account might serve as a textbook case). But instead of patiently waiting for the convulsive, liberating phenomenon to display itself, the screamer forestalls it from the first beat, leading to a self-denial of his only remaining outlet. Anyone who has seen Adriano Celentano in performance will recall the muscular spasms that alter his face and persona completely when he sings. He perfectly mimics the early warning signs of a seizure, though the actual attack never arrives, but lasts it out, so to speak, in a dormant cramplike condition. The screamer would like to take a sort of revenge against the industrialized society by regressing, at least in his intentions, to a primitive state. That "noble savage," however, that he wants to reawaken in himself comes to life with all the neurotic symptoms of modern man—incapable, by his very alienation, of true spontaneity. And out of this comes the tragic fixity of the screamer's song.

In one guise, even the syncopated works of yesterday offered something like this. A divide, similar to the one between screamers and crooners, already existed in the landscape of Italian popular song in the years between 1939 and 1943. That time saw the escalation of polemics between devotees of Rabagliati, Bonino and Natalino Otto—the exponents of the "American style"—and champions of classic "Italian-style" works by Othello Boccaccini and Oscar Carboni, among others. With its jazzy origins, syncopated music came wrapped in an aura of "primitivism," even if this was rather domesticated. Yet there as well, despite the rhythmic twitches, the tuneful spasms, the frequent restatements of musical phrases, no "unprompted" event overtook the performance. The "frenzy" was limited to skimming across the syncope within the confines of the beat, where the energy was built up and released whenever the time signature was marked and consequently sidestepped. The gestures best suited to express jazz's effects on mind and body were the mechanical tapping of feet, the hebephrenic wobbling of the head. All the same, there a certain phenomenon of "internal uplift" occurred, which no longer appears in the songs we are examining, where the "paralysis" is almost absolute. Syncopated music, while breaking up the primordial arc into many short, serial convulsions, still allowed its participants the ersatz feeling of free movement within the boundaries of society's cage, a certain margin of independence at their disposal. And indeed this explains why jazz caught on so deeply in American culture before becoming a more commercialized form of expression: with its innocuous frenzies, it nicely conveyed the limits put aside for individual freedoms by a society set on making human rights coexist beside a program involving the total leveling of tastes and mores. The consumer of syncopated music appears as the model everyman for a world ready to give every guarantee of personal liberty, so long as he keeps to the rules of communal life; he shows how to have fun while remaining in his assigned place. Whatever his area of work or struggle is in reality, in musical terms it translates to the martial beat in 2/2, a rigid barrier that the Italian scions of "jazz" never tried to cross.

Of course, the champions of jazziness carried a good measure of resignation. No spirit of revolt against their social debasement seeped out of their tunes, which if anything expressed jolly approval. The figure of the U.S. Marine in Korea, who spends his breaks from active combat listening to jazz on his radio while flashing an optimistic smile, has become classic. There could not be a better image to articulate the submission of the individual to the social system into which he is inserted.

ⓔⓧⓓ

"Before the word became a means to communicate," says Otto Fenichel,* "the activities of the organs of speech had a purely libidinous discharge." That axiom measures well against the spirit of those songs, but perhaps even better against the little cries and gestures that typify certain renditions of today's screamer tunes. The "scream" isn't always a re-creation of primordial, barbaric desires. Often enough, when the performers are called Mina or Jenny Luna, their persona appears to the listener's imagination with the accent and demeanor of a child: a counterfeit nurseling whose gluttony isn't set on candy bars or lollipops, but the sexual morsels of adulthood. The disciples of the scream, prone as if facing the anonymous altar of Sex, and who seem ready to say that

---

* Otto Fenichel, *Trattato di psicoanalisi delle nevrosi e delle psicosi*, Rome: Astrolabio, 1951, p. 355.

they have found a sort of all-purpose panacea in this deity, fall back on all the tricks and cantrips they can muster so they can worship undisturbed. So the voice of childhood, the epitome of innocence, becomes the screen behind which the listener takes refuge without the hassles of his conscience: a voice that corrupts him and all the while absolves him in a climate of Arcadian debauchery.

It's hard to say whether it's better to remain the serfs of an organized industrial society rather than fall into an anarchy of instincts. Whatever the case, the screamers' fan base, instead of resigning themselves to their condition of alienation, as fans of syncopated music did in their own time, seem to present themselves as men in revolt, with their hands waving the banner of Sex like a battle standard of freedom. A curious fantasy indeed, seeing that it reduces all of their emancipatory demands to something that, as long as social mutilation continues and no real effort is made to surmount it, they will never reach: the heights of a satisfied love. Yet it's likely that anyone keen on the screamer genre is only seeking a kind of analytical pleasure out of sex, a voyeuristic sea change from the visual sphere to the auditory. Incapable, due to his unripe spirit, of reaching a full image of love occurring, the consumer of screamer songs shrinks back, centering his attention on specific, fragmentary descriptions of the reality to which he would aspire; and the screams would be an attempt—certainly in vain—to instill heat into those frigid descriptions. Why else spend so much energy, such peristaltic emphasis, on underlining what's already too easily clear?

Translator's Acknowledgments

I am especially grateful to Luca Signorelli for many months of valued feedback; to Andrea Signorelli for an unforgettable tour of central Turin; to Sonia Gianotti for her help in locating the author's estate; to Michael Pollak for assistance in checking the novel's Robert Musil sample against the original German; to the novel's original publisher, Mr. Stefano Jacini, for a helpful reply to my queries; to John and Katherine Dolan for listening to an early draft; to Mr. Emilio Jona (the original "Attorney Segre") for his vivid recollections of Giorgio De Maria's extraordinary life; to the author's children, Corallina and Domenico, for their hospitality and support; and to my superb editorial team of Katie Adams, Dave Cole and Gina Iaquinta.

Finally, my commissioning editor, Will Menaker, deserves eternal thanks (and infamy) for his part in resuscitating the Library and "connecting it across the ether" to its new, English-speaking audience!

GIORGIO DE MARIA (1924–2009) was a novelist, pianist, critic and songwriter. Born and raised in Turin, he held the post of theater reviewer for *L'Unità*—the radical newspaper formed by Antonio Gramsci—from 1958 to 1965. Alongside figures such as Sergio Liberovici, Italo Calvino, Michele Straniero and Emilio Jona, he cofounded the avant-garde music group Cantacronache, without which, Umberto Eco reminisced, "the history of the Italian song would have been very different." Remembered for his savage humor and astute eye for horror, De Maria authored numerous short stories and theater works alongside a teleplay and four novels, the most acclaimed of which is his cult classic *The Twenty Days of Turin* (1977).

RAMON GLAZOV is a journalist, critic and author of fiction. He has written for a range of U.S. and Australian publications, including *Jacobin*, the *Monthly*, the *Saturday Paper*, *Overland Literary Journal* and *Tincture Journal*.